Check Mate

Leah Brunner

Leah Brunner Publishing

Contents

To my brother, Luke. Thank you for helping me with my math homework growing up. (Well, more so, getting frustrated with my inability to calculate equations, and then doing it for me).

Not all heroes wear capes.

Chapter One

David

I loathe surprises.

You always hear people say things like, "I can't decide. Surprise me!"

I'm convinced those people have some kind of diagnosable mental condition. Who wouldn't want to plan for any situation and know exactly what to expect?

Not me. No, thank you. Surprises are for people who love chaos.

I'm currently standing outside the front door of my craftsman-style home, and despite how sturdy and structurally sound it is… I do not want to step through that front door.

"Why?" one might ask. It's because today is my thirtieth birthday, and I happen to know my family is inside, waiting to surprise me.

The Windells aren't known for their ability to be sneaky or keep secrets. No, our family is known for being flawless. Good looks, magnificent brains, charismatic personalities. We have it all... well, everyone except me.

I'm the only dull one in the family. The crooked screw, the squeaky wheel. You know those activities in children's magazines where you find the item that doesn't belong? Well, that's me, I'm the item.

A familiar meow coming from behind me interrupts my thoughts. I don't even have to turn my head to know my next-door neighbor's gigantic cat is sitting on my porch steps.

"Not today, cat."

Meow.

I heave a heavy sigh and force myself to grasp the doorknob and turn it. At least going inside will get me away from this stupid cat. I open the front door gingerly, bracing myself for impact. I can feel my body stiffen as I wait for people to jump out and scream at me.

"SURPRISE!"

The light flicks on, illuminating my living room. My family fills the space; everyone is wearing party hats and they've blown confetti all over my immaculate floors.

My jaw clenches and I close my eyes for a second to compose myself before opening them again and forcing myself to smile and ignore the mess. "Wow, thanks, guys."

My sister, Sophie, appears from behind her giant of a husband, Drew. Her blonde hair is braided down her back, and she's wearing a yellow sundress that's as sunny as her personality. "We got you! I knew you'd be surprised."

"Yep." I shrug one shoulder. "You got me good."

Drew's brown eyes meet mine, and he gives me a knowing look as if to say, *"Thanks for playing along."* We've become pretty close since he married my sister, and he can read me pretty well. "You want a drink?" He asks.

"Please." I nod my thanks to him.

My younger brother, Brooks, and older brother, Madden, embrace me in brotherly hugs and back pats. They have the signature Windell looks with blonde hair and blue eyes. They're pretty much carbon copies of our father. Madden is dressed professionally in dress pants and a polo, which is actually pretty casual for him. Meanwhile, Brooks is wearing distressed jeans with a vintage tee and backward ball cap.

"Happy birthday, bro," Brooks says with a mischievous smirk on his face. "I know how you *love* surprises."

Madden laughs. "Yeah… Mom and Sophie couldn't be stopped," he whispers with a grimace.

My mom runs toward me, shoving my brothers out of her way. For a tiny woman, she packs a punch. I got my dark hair from my mom but thankfully inherited my dad's height. "My sweet David!" She pulls me into a bear hug. "Happy thirtieth birthday."

Dad comes around to my other side and wraps his arms around me so I'm sandwiched between the two of them. "Happy birthday, Son," he says as he pulls away.

"We're so proud of you," Mom tells me, her blue eyes glossing over with tears.

Dad wraps an arm around my mom. "Come on, Diane. Let's get you a cocktail." Dad winks at me as he leads her away.

Drew comes from the kitchen with a glass of bourbon in his hand and hands it to me just as my nieces and nephews bombard me and wrap themselves around my ankles.

"Uncle David! Happy birfday!" little Samantha tells me with her lisp.

Drew's daughter, Penny, who's now Samantha's big sister, corrects her: "BirTH-day," she says, enunciating the *th* sound.

Penny places both hands on her hips and looks me over. "So, you're thirty, huh?"

"Yes, ma'am."

Her eyebrows raise slightly. "Gettin' pretty old."

Drew overhears his daughter and rushes over and hoists her over his shoulder. "That's enough out of you. Thirty is *not* old. I'm way older than that!" Samantha runs after them.

My two nephews are still attached to my ankles. Their blonde heads look up at me with smirks on their adorable faces. It's like seeing Madden and Brooks reincarnated.

Lord, help us all.

Oliver glances around the room before whispering, "Hey Uncle David, can you tell them you're ready for cake? Mom says we can't have it until you say so."

I glance at my sister-in-law, Odette, who rolls her eyes at her son. Kids are loud whisperers, so the entire room could easily hear his request.

I shuffle my way toward the kitchen, where I'm assuming the cake is, when I spot a large poster of a man tacked up on my living room wall. It looks like they have painted clothing on him, and he's holding a calculator.

Sophie comes up behind me, laughing. "Pin the calculator on the accountant."

"I see that." I shake my head, but can't help the smile that tugs at my lips. "But did he used to be naked?"

Odette appears at my other side. "Um yeah... we got it at a shop online for bachelorette parties."

Sophie stifles a giggle. "Let's just say he previously didn't have clothing... or calculators..."

Oliver releases himself from my leg and studies the poster. "Why was he naked? And what would you pin to him if there weren't calculators, Mommy?"

Odette rolls her lips together to keep from laughing. "Umm... So, how about that cake?"

Sophie and Odette erupt into laughter. I sigh and bend down to pick up my youngest nephew, Bradford. He's only a year and a half and not talking much yet, so he's currently my favorite. He cuddles into me and I lay my chin against his fuzzy blonde head as I walk into the kitchen to find the birthday cake. They covered my large kitchen island with an array of desserts. There are several flavors of pie, cupcakes, sugar cookies decorated to look like calculators, and a giant birthday cake that's frosted to resemble a W-2 tax form.

I chuckle, amused at how much thought my sister put into this. Sophie sidles up next to me with a big grin. "You like it?"

"As far as surprise parties go, this one isn't so bad." I playfully bump her shoulder with my own.

"I'll take that as a yes." She winks and then walks around to the other side of the island to get a cake knife. "Who's ready for cake?" She yells loud enough for everyone in the next room to hear.

All four children appear in the kitchen seemingly from out of nowhere and scream, "me, me!" Oh, and also Brooks. Because he's basically a child.

Brooks picks up Samantha and Oliver and chants with them. He's the fun uncle. Don't get me wrong; I love being an uncle way more than I thought I would. My nieces and nephews are hilarious... I'm just not going to get on the floor and let them play "horsey."

Once everyone is in the kitchen, I'm forced to listen to them serenade me with the happy birthday song. Then we dig into the desserts.

I have a weakness for chocolate, so I select a chocolate calculator cookie and sink my teeth into it and sigh. Brooks claps me on the back, nearly causing me to choke on my cookie.

I cough a few times and he chuckles. "So, you're thirty, single, and boring." He smirks, and I notice he has frosting on his upper lip but I don't tell him.

Madden is sitting at the bar a few feet from us feeding Bradford cake and laughs at Brooks' comment. "Isn't it thirty, flirty, and thriving?"

"David isn't boring!" Sophie defends me before shoving a bite of pie into her mouth.

Brooks scoffs. "Are you kidding me? He's the most predictable person I've ever met."

"It's called *consistent*, Brooks," I deadpan.

He shrugs. "Sure. But doesn't it bother you that in thirty years of life you've done nothing exciting or out of the ordinary?"

His comments are hitting home and he doesn't even realize it. He thinks he's just jesting, but it actually *does* bother me. I'm thirty and have never even left the United States. I'm constantly reading about other countries and watching travel documentaries... but I can never convince myself to book a flight. What if the beds are uncomfortable? Or the flights are turbulent? Or the food. What if I hate it?

Leaving the comforts of home seems daunting. Traveling via documentaries is much safer.

I can't even remember the last time I took time off work and went on a proper vacation.

I take a large bite of my cookie to disguise my facial expression, then wash it down with some bourbon. Note to self: cookies and bourbon do not complement each other.

My brother-in-law, Drew, pipes up. "There's nothing wrong with being comfortable and content."

Am I content though? Comfortable yes, steady yes, boring... yes.

Brooks smirks at me. "Yeah, I suppose so. If David ever does something out of the ordinary, I'll run through the streets naked." He laughs.

Drew and Madden perk up at his comment. "Really?" Drew asks, crossing his arms.

Madden mirrors his movement. "Yeah, are we betting on this?"

Brooks rolls his eyes. "Okay, sure. I'll take that bet."

"I've actually been thinking about doing a bit of traveling," I tell them, trying to conceal my smile.

Brooks raises a brow. "If you do anything out of the ordinary before Christmas, I'll run through the streets nude. But, if you *don't...* you have to go skydiving with me."

I calculate for a moment. It's August 25th now, so that gives me several months to think of something.

"You're on, but I have something better in mind than you running around naked. Nobody wants to see that, anyway."

"That's definitely not true... but what do you have in mind?" Brooks crosses his arms and eyes me curiously.

"If you lose the bet, you'll go four months without dating." I thrust my hand out in front of me.

He bites his bottom lip as he contemplates my terms. "Fine. Since you're going to lose the bet, it really doesn't matter."

Madden jumps between us before Brooks and I can shake on it. "Wait, what's the consequence if Brooks loses and doesn't hold up his end of the agreement?"

Drew hums and nods in agreement. "Yeah, I don't trust him."

Brooks grins mischievously, showing off the dimples in his cheeks that have long gotten him out of trouble. "I know, I know... it's hard to believe women could resist me for four entire months."

Madden, Drew, and I roll our eyes in unison.

"Alright," I start. "Since you so generously gave me the idea." I smirk at Brooks. "If we catch you on a date with a woman, kissing a woman, or even holding a woman's hand before the four months are up… you'll run naked through the Lady's Annual Spring Garden Party at the country club."

The set of Brooks' shoulders exudes unadulterated confidence… but the slow descent of his Adam's apple as he gulps gives his true feelings away.

He laughs, but it sounds forced. "Isn't Mom on the planning committee for the garden party? And all of her friends?"

I nod my head, and a smile slowly creeps across my face.

"We'd make sure Mom wasn't there to witness your demise." Madden reassures him. "But there's nothing we can do about her friends."

Brooks shrugs and extends his hand to seal the deal. "I'm not too worried."

I narrow my eyes at him before I grab his hand, and we seal our fates with a firm shake.

Madden and Drew look on with excitement in their eyes. They'll be entertained either way, but I'm going to make sure Brooks loses this bet.

My doorbell rings, and Odette goes to answer it. A few seconds later, Odette enters the room with my annoying neighbor, Isabella Romero. I close my eyes and curse under my breath. Why did she invite this woman into my house? The more she knows about me, the better she can retaliate in our ongoing neighbor pranks.

Okay, *pranks* is putting it nicely.

I cock my head to the side and widen my eyes at my sister-in-law. Trying to convey my disapproval of her letting in an unwanted visitor. Isabella has never been inside my home, and I wanted to keep it that way.

Everyone's attention turns to the petite woman now standing in my kitchen. Brooks, Madden and Drew all glance at her then turn their attention on me. Their eyes are wide and amused. Isabella is wearing short denim cutoffs and a loose t-shirt that's short, so her tanned stomach peeks out when she moves. She has her long black hair piled up on top of her head in a big, loose bun.

She's an attractive woman, I'll give her that. But she's still annoying as hell... I bet she's one of those chaotic people who loves surprises.

She glances around the room, taking in my family, who are all abnormally quiet at the moment. "I'm so sorry for interrupting your party, but I was wondering if you've seen Mo? For reasons unknown... he seems drawn to you."

"Your cat's name is Mo?" I ask, wondering where she came up with such a ridiculous name.

Her lips form a straight line as if trying to conceal her annoyance in front of my family. "Well, at first I thought he was a girl and named him Moana... but then the vet told me he's a... he. So I shortened it to Mo."

I try to keep a straight face... I really do. But my mouth won't cooperate and turns up in a smirk. "You insulted his manhood, and you're confused why he likes me better than you? Seems self-explanatory."

Isabella's eyes turn hard and murderous, but she forces a smile on her pretty face. "Thanks for clearing that up for me. Now, have you seen him?"

Noticing her eyes dancing around the room again, taking my home in and probably making mental notes on how to make my life more miserable, I narrow my eyes at her. "He was on my porch earlier, but I haven't seen him since."

She meets my steely gaze and lifts her chin like she's trying to appear bigger than she actually is. I want to laugh at the thought. This woman is the chihuahua to my German Shepherd. She has to be at least a foot shorter than me.

A loud meow interrupts our stare-down. We both look in the direction the sound came from and see the cat in question meandering down the hallway toward us like this is his home.

I scrub a hand down my face with a groan. "How did he get in here?" I direct the question to Brooks since he's the troublemaker.

He throws his hands up in defense. "I opened your bedroom window earlier to let some fresh air in... Odette changed a dirty diaper back there and the stench was awful."

My eyes flick to Odette, and she rolls her eyes. Mo walks toward me and rubs himself against my legs while he purrs loudly.

Isabella smiles. "Wow, he really likes you."

"Great. Just what I wanted." I cross my arms and quirk a brow. "Was there anything else you needed? Besides a basic feline anatomy lesson?"

She opens her mouth to speak, but Brooks interrupts her. "Do you want some birthday cake? There's plenty!"

I shoot a glare in his direction and he grins back at me.

She glances at me briefly, just long enough for me to see the defiance in her gaze. "Sure, I'd *love* some cake."

Her tongue peeks out to wet her lips as she eyes the desserts on my kitchen island. This draws my attention to her full, dark-pink lips, which give her the appearance of having a constant pout. Which is contradictory to what I've seen of her personality so far. Whenever she interacts with the mail lady or her sisters—at least I'm assuming they're her sisters because they all look alike—she's all charming smiles with an easy way about her, like she doesn't have a care in the world. Until she talks to me... then she's not so smiley.

Sophie cuts a big slice of cake and hands it to her with a smile. "It's David's thirtieth birthday today!"

Isabella's big brown eyes twinkle with mischief. "Only thirty? I thought you were much older."

The kitchen fills with my family's laughter at her comment. Her effortless charm and witty comebacks have even my own family enraptured. Maybe if she didn't live next door to me, I'd like her more...

"He's always acted much older than he is, ever since he was a child," my mom tells her.

Brooks swings an arm around Isabella's shoulder, which makes me feel an unwanted prickle of annoyance. I can't pinpoint why it annoys me, but it's *definitely* not jealousy.

"Yep, he's always been a boring, old goodie-two-shoes," Brooks tells her with a chuckle.

I use my thumb and index finger to adjust my glasses. "I believe the word you're looking for is responsible."

"That's exactly right," Mom says as she sidles up next to me and loops her arm through mine. She briefly wrinkles her nose at Mo, who's still rubbing against my legs. My mother has always been very against animals living indoors. "My David is the most responsible, safe, consistent person I know."

"Which could also be described as predictable, mundane, and vanilla," Brooks retorts before winking at Isabella.

My nostrils flare and I feel my face heat with frustration, or maybe annoyance. I'm not sure what's triggering this reaction. Brooks and I roast each other constantly. Perhaps it's because Isabella's in my house.

It's definitely *not* the fact that Brooks is flirting with her.

Isabella finishes her cake and walks toward me to pick up her cat. Mo is a large cat, most likely a Maine Coon. I may have googled cat breeds out of curiosity. He's fluffy and orange with light orange stripes. Like a baby tiger. He looks huge in her arms. Her small stature makes him seem even larger than normal.

"Thank you for the cake. I need to get this guy back home." She nuzzles him with her nose. "Yes I do," she baby talks to Mo.

I sigh and withhold an eye roll. "On your walk back, why don't you stop and trim the English ivy creeping up on my side of the fence?"

"Sorry, I would... but for some strange reason, my beautiful English ivy shriveled up and died. Almost makes me wonder if someone sprayed them with poison?" she says sarcastically, then gives me an accusatory glance.

I keep my expression neutral but feel secretly satisfied that the English ivy died... in my defense; I was only trying to kill the ivy on *my* side of the fence, but the entire plant keeled over. And I'm not a monster... I didn't spray poison on them because I wasn't sure if it would hurt Mo. *Ugh, I cannot get used to that name.* Vinegar worked just fine—perhaps a little too well.

Isabella turns to leave. Before she's out of eyesight, she stops and looks at me over her shoulder. "Oh, and happy birthday, David."

As soon as we hear the front door close, my family explodes with comments and questions about the tiny spawn of Satan, who lives next door to me.

"Duuuuuude! You never mentioned she was a smoke show," Brooks says, then fans himself like he's on fire.

Sophie chimes in, "Yeah, even I can admit she's hot."

Odette nods in agreement. "She also seems really sweet!"

Drew and Madden are quiet, but they're smirking at me like they know something I don't.

"What?" I ask Madden, irritated at his smug face.

He rolls his lips together like he's trying not to smile. "You like her."

"He totally does," Drew agrees.

Rolling my eyes, I walk over to the cake and serve myself a big slice, then use a plastic fork to shove a big bite into my mouth. I close my eyes and savor the sweetness. But once my eyes are closed, my neighbor's eyes pop into my mind, the same color as the chocolate I love so much. I groan. Now she's ruining chocolate for me, too!

The only way to cure my irritation is more chocolate. Lots of chocolate.

Odette rattles something from across the room, getting our attention. "If you don't like her, then what are these?"

I look at the container she's holding that's clearly labeled *cat treats*.

Everyone waits for me to answer. I take my time chewing and swallowing the cake, trying to come up with a suitable answer.

"Her cat always seems to end up inside my house… how else would I get him *out* than by enticing him with treats?"

Odette sets the container back inside the cabinet she found them in and crosses her arms. "But why take the time to label them?"

I walk over to the cabinet and open both doors for everyone to see. The shelves are lined with glass containers, each one with a matching label. "Everything in my pantry has a label."

Sophie walks over and peeks inside the cabinet. "Wow. Can you organize our pantry next?"

"Fine," I tell her with an annoyed sigh. But I love using my label maker, so I don't really mind.

Brooks grabs a cookie and takes a bite. "I dunno, Soph," he says around the cookie. "He's going to be awfully busy doing all that unpredictable stuff."

"Brooks!" Mom hands him a napkin and grabs the cookie out of his hand. "Use your manners."

I withhold a groan and wonder when I can kick them all out without coming across as rude. All I want to do is enjoy my birthday in my clean, quiet house and watch a documentary while sipping some bourbon.

The annoying thing is, they're not completely wrong... I don't *like* Isabella, but I can't deny her beauty. What hot-blooded male could?

But in my thirty years of life on this earth, I've never met a woman I could tolerate enough to spend over one evening with, and Isabella Romero definitely will not change that. I don't dislike all people... but my circle is small, and I like it that way.

Plus, women like changing things. And I like my orderly life... and my organized pantry.

Chapter Two

Isabella

I scratch Mo behind the ears as I carry him back over to my house. "Why are you so smitten with Mr. Grumpy Pants, anyway?"

I open the front door to my little rental house, which isn't nearly as well-maintained as my neighbor's. But it's my own, and I love it. Even though my infuriatingly traditional parents didn't think I should move out until I got married.

I set Mo down and close the door behind me. He instantly runs to the door and starts scratching at it like he wants to go back to David's house.

"Mo Catson Romero... you're a traitor." He plops down in front of the door and rolls over onto his back. I ignore his begging and walk to my small floral couch and sit down. It's a hand-me-down from my parents, but it's comfortable.

David's annoyed expression flashes in my mind. He'd be so handsome if he smiled once in a while. And what's up with his abnormally perfect family? Are they secret vampires like the Cullens from Twilight or something?

I pick up my laptop to continue the post I was creating for my travel website, Isa's Itinerary. A documentary about the Inca Empire is playing quietly in the background for inspiration, but I'm too distracted to focus on the documentary *or* my website.

I can't help but glance around my small house and compare it to David's. His house is masculine with wood floors that are perfectly polished... just like the man himself. His simple leather furniture is minimalistic, but looks rich and luxurious at the same time. Meanwhile, my house is a little run-down—shabby-chic, if you will. I love my colorful vintage style, but after being in my neighbor's house for the first time, my house seems a little childish and cluttered.

I cross my arms and frown. How did he manage to make me feel bad about my entire life after just five minutes of interaction?

My sister Rosa waltzes through the front door without knocking. My sisters know they never have to knock. It's our rule.

She walks across the room and then flops down on the couch next to me. "Oh my gosh, are you watching another documentary about Machu Picchu?"

"I want to learn as much as possible before I visit! Plus, it's our heritage."

Rosa rolls her eyes. "You and your genealogy results. I don't get why you're so obsessive about it." Rosa has made fun of me incessantly since I took a DNA test last year and found out we're actually only 85% Mexican and 15% Incan. She swears it's incorrect and there's no way that's true.

Turning off the TV, I stand to get myself a glass of water from the kitchen, which isn't that far away since my house is small. "I wouldn't say obsessed. I'd say... fascinated."

She follows me into the kitchen with a smirk. "You've never seemed as fascinated about Mexico as you are about Peru."

Cocking my head to the side, I give her an annoyed stare. She knows how proud I am of our Mexican heritage, and how much I looked forward to our trips to Guadalajara with Abuela. Those trips with her, exploring the city where she was born, were some of my most precious memories and instilled in me a love of travel.

"You know I'm proud to be Mexican-American. I love our art and culture... and don't even get me started on the food. But there's an entire world out there to explore! I already know everything there is to know about our history. Mama and Papa have practically made us memorize the family tree."

She gives me a sympathetic nod. "I know, Bella. I was only teasing."

I smile at her before opening the kitchen cabinet, so she knows I'm not upset. The cabinet door creaks like it always does, but I ignore it and grab a clean glass. The kitchen has off-white cabinets and laminate countertops that are supposed to look like marble—but don't quite pull it off. I like that my house is older and feels like a cottage, and it's just big enough for me and my cat—the cat that was supposed to be the embodiment of my free-spirit and need to have adventure... aka Moana. Oh well, I love Mo anyway.

And my house doesn't have to be as fancy as David's for me to love it, too.

"Why are you scowling?" Rosa asks, taking the glass from my hand and turning to fill it with water from the tap.

I hadn't realized I was scowling... ugh, I'm turning into my neighbor. "Nothing, just anxious about my trip," I lie, then take a sip of water. "You know, it's not too late for you to come with me... they still have a few spots left." I slide the travel pamphlet that's laying on my counter towards her.

She quirks a brow and slides the pamphlet back toward me. "Yeah, hiking fifty miles up to some old ruins isn't really my thing."

"It's only forty-seven miles."

She sighs and Mo jumps up on the countertop and plops down right on top of the pamphlet. Rosa laughs. "See? Even Mo doesn't want me to go." She pets him a few times and he purrs. "Besides, I need to stay back and take care of him for you."

"Good point."

She looks at me with a twinkle in her eye. "Maybe you'll meet a guy on the trip. Someone into hiking and looking at really old stuff."

I bat my eyelashes playfully. "It's always been my dream to find a man who loves old stuff!"

We both laugh and take our water into the living room and sit on the couch side by side. Rosa breaks the silence with a grimace on her face. "Speaking of your future husband..."

"Oh jeez, what now?"

"Mama invited a man to come into the restaurant tomorrow night. They think if they give you his table you two will fall in love and not know they had anything to do with it." She wrinkles her nose and looks away from me.

I close my eyes and take a deep breath. My temper will not help the situation. "Their meddling is out of control. I'm twenty-eight and they act like I'm a spinster!"

"Well, you do live alone with your cat," she teases.

I shove her, but can't hide my smirk at her comment. "Shut up... you're next, you know."

"Psh, they have to marry you off first since you're the oldest."

I release a heavy sigh. "There's so much to do and explore before I settle down. I don't know why they're in such a hurry."

"Sorry, Sis." Rosa glances at the laptop I set on the sofa earlier and then looks at me with a sympathetic gaze. "Have you talked to Mama and Papa anymore about cutting back your hours at the restaurant?"

I slump back into the couch cushions. "Not since that failure of a conversation a few weeks back." I rest a hand on the laptop sitting next to me. It's the life source of all my dreams. "They think my website is some silly little blog."

"That sucks. I know you've worked really hard on it." She sighs. "But you know them... the family legacy..."

"I know." I rest my head on the couch and look up at the ceiling. "They want to give me roots, when all my heart longs for is wings."

Rosa rests her head on my shoulder. "Sorry to cut our conversation short, but I have to get to the restaurant. I'm closing tonight."

"That's alright. Don't let our parents marry you off during your shift."

We laugh and say our goodbyes. She gives me a hug and Mo a pat on the head on her way out.

Once she's gone and I'm left alone in my quiet house with only my thoughts, I decide not to let my parent's expectations get me down. I'm leaving for Peru in two weeks, crossing another place off of my travel list.

I glance around my small but open living space, seeing my Eiffel Tower figurine from Paris, and the framed photo I took of the Empire State Building in New York. These are just a few of the reminders I need that I don't need a lot of money, fancy things, luxurious leather couches... *or* a husband. If I just keep working on my website, I can continue earning enough to cover my travel expenses and this little house. Just me and Mo against the world—er, my parents.

The following evening, I walk into the large breakroom at Abuela's, my parent's restaurant. I'm wearing my least flattering black pants and an ill-fitting white button-up. Basically, you can barely even tell I'm a woman. I also made sure not to put any makeup on and braided my hair into pigtails.

What can I say? I ugly up pretty well.

I lock my purse and belongings into my locker and then sign-in on the iPad system we installed five years ago when my Abuela passed and Mama and Papa took over the restaurant. When I turn to leave, I almost run right into my mother.

She takes me in with a look of horror on her face. "Isabella! No, no, no. Porque te pones asi?"

Ugh, this isn't good. She only speaks in Spanish when she's mad. I decide to play dumb. "What's the matter? Black pants, white shirt. True to our required uniform."

"My sweet Bella, you always look so lovely, even for work. But this?" She puts one hand on her curvy hip and flails her other around in mid-air like she can't decide what to gesture at first.

She doesn't know that Rosa told me about the guy coming in tonight, so I continue with this little charade she thinks she's pulling off. "I'm sorry it's not my nicest outfit, but it's my night to work in the kitchen, so I didn't think it would be a big deal."

I hold her gaze, the same big brown eyes as my own, waiting to see if she caves. Instead, she stands up a little straighter and grabs my wrist, yanking me from the office and then down the hallway and into the large kitchen. This is my favorite space in the restaurant; it's all stainless steel and organized, but grab some spices and veggies and the possibilities are endless. I love how creative you can be while cooking. Our chef, Marco, waves at me and I wave back with my free hand.

My mother lets go of me and grabs a black apron from the hook on the wall. She throws it over my neck and then ties the strings around my waist so tight I can barely breathe.

"We're short-staffed tonight, Bella. You'll have to wait tables instead of working in the kitchen." She pauses to look me over. "Did you bring any makeup?"

"Um, no. I wasn't supposed to be waitressing tonight."

She mutters something under her breath in Spanish. "Well, nothing more can be done. Start with the back corner tables." She exits the double doors with a heavy sigh.

Marco looks at me with a sympathetic expression. "What was that all about?" he whispers, looking at the double doors like Mama has superhuman hearing. Honestly, she probably does.

"You don't even want to know." I grab one of the tablets we take orders on from the charging station next to the double doors, and head out to meet the man who will most definitely *not* be my future husband.

As I walk toward the back corner of the restaurant, I take in my surroundings. My family's restaurant is nostalgic for me. Although Abuela's has been in the same location since my grandparents opened it forty years ago, my parents have completely changed it since taking over. It used to have ugly red carpet, and the walls were adorned with colorful sombreros. Mama and Papa modernized it so the ambiance matched the amazing Mexican cuisine. The walls are now stucco with colorful paintings of flowers native to Mexico, and the floors are light brown tiles. We even installed more windows to bring in light. The restaurant has really taken off since they remodeled five years ago.

Weekends are the busiest, of course, so it's a full house tonight. I smile at the other servers, noting that our usual Saturday evening staff is here... meaning we aren't actually short-staffed. Just as I suspected.

One server, Courtney, walks toward me with a smile. She's blonde and has a bubbly personality, which makes her great with the customers. She leans in to whisper, "Did Rosa warn you?"

I sigh. "Yep."

Courtney grimaces and pats me on the shoulder. She's probably close to my parents' age, but she's worked here so long she feels like a big sister. The staff all feel like part of the family, and I enjoy working here. But if I wasn't working at the restaurant so much, I'd have more time to dedicate to building my website and getting sponsorships.

I continue walking around the tables, smiling at any customers looking my way. Finally, I make it to the back corner. There's a man alone in the corner booth, looking at his leather-bound menu. His white linen shirt looks nice against his brown skin but is unbuttoned one too many buttons, exposing his furry chest. I bet he told my parents he's Catholic, maybe even hung some rosary beads on his rear-view mirror for good measure.

I wish I knew what vehicle he drives so I could go out to the parking lot and see if I'm right.

I'm sure this man isn't a horrible person, but the fact that he's in on this scheme with my parents makes me instantly dislike him.

Stepping close to his table, I clear my throat. "Good evening. I'm Isabella and I'll be your server this evening."

He smiles up at me with decent-enough teeth and brown eyes. "Well hello, I'm Fabio. Nice to meet you, Isabella."

Fabio? My parents really want me to marry someone named Fabio? Yikes.

"Can I start you off with something to drink?" I smile, keeping our interaction professional.

"Sure! What do you recommend? What's *your* favorite beverage?"

I decide to have a little fun with him. "I love our margaritas, just don't have too many or you'll end up dancing on the table with your top off... I had to learn that the hard way."

His eyebrows shoot up and then furrow in concern. "Oh dear. Thanks for the warning."

I bite the insides of my cheeks to hold in my laughter.

"I think I'll just have water for now."

"Good choice. I'll be right back with that." I spin on my heel and walk toward the kitchen. As soon as I'm through the double doors, I allow myself to laugh.

My youngest sister, Lily, is in the kitchen now and stares at me with a bemused expression. "What's so funny?"

She's chopping vegetables for Marco and wearing a white apron. Her dark hair is pulled back in a French braid. She looks youthful and adorable as always. I walk over to her and give her a kiss on the cheek.

"Nothing, just having a little fun." I wink.

She smirks. "Does this have anything to do with Mama switching our duties for the evening?"

I laugh. "Maybe..."

Walking across the kitchen, I grab a glass and fill it with ice and water, then head back out to Fabio's table.

"Here's that water, sir."

He smiles and takes a sip of water. "Thank you, please call me Fabio."

I nod my head. "Are you ready to order, or do you need some more time?"

"I was actually wanting your input. What's good here?" he asks, holding eye contact too long.

I bite my bottom lip while I think. "Well, that depends... if you're congested, I'd recommend our spicy chimichanga. But if you're having digestive trouble... our burrito platter could solve that right away."

His mouth gapes open for a second before he snaps it closed. Mission accomplished.

"Excuse us, Fabio." Mama appears out of nowhere and puts her hands on my shoulders. "I need to have a word with my daughter." She smiles politely at Fabio, then spins me in the kitchen's direction and basically pushes me the rest of the way.

We go through the double doors and she whirls around, her eyes wide in outrage. "What are you doing out there??"

I shrug. "Trying to be a good server?"

"By asking him about his digestion?!"

I hear Lily snicker behind us. Mama glares at her and she goes back to chopping vegetables.

Papa enters the room from the back door, probably coming from his office. He's wearing a green polo with the Abuela's logo on it and dress pants. His brown eyes go wide as he sees me and Mama arguing. He attempts to sneak back out until I narrow my eyes at him. He grimaces before cautiously walking up behind Mama and placing a hand on her back.

"Tranquila, mi amor. Let's calm down," he tells Mama in his soothing voice.

She snaps her head to look at him. "I *am* calm!" Then she turns her angry gaze back to me. "You're ruining this on purpose, aren't you?"

I bring my hand to my chest. "Whatever do you mean?"

"Don't play dumb. It's obvious Rosa told you. Fabio is a very nice man, Bella." She takes a deep breath and gives Papa a pat on the cheek. "Give him a chance. I just want you to be happy like me and your Papa."

"I know. But you've got to stop with the meddling." I look between my parents and my father looks as guilty as my mother. "*Both* of you! I never know when some random guy is going to show up and try to marry me."

"You're being dramatic." Mama rolls her eyes. "Go back out there and be your normal, charming self and we can forget this ever happened."

I place a fist on my hip. "And then you'll stop trying to set me up?"

"I was married and already had two children by the time I was twenty-eight, you know."

"Mama..."

She crosses her arms. "Fine. I'll stop trying to set you up. But no more talking about bodily functions to customers."

"Deal." I turn to leave the kitchen.

Papa calls out, "We love you, Bella!" as I'm leaving.

Chapter Three

David

It's Saturday, the day after my birthday, and I'm glad to have the party over with so I can get back to my normal routine.

I open my front door to retrieve my newspaper—yes, I still subscribe to a newspaper. Social media is the worst. I prefer getting my news the old-fashioned way—and, of course, Isabella's cat is sitting on my porch.

I sigh, and he greets me with a meow. With a quick glance around the quiet neighborhood, I bend down and pat him on the head. He purrs and leans into my hand.

My lips quirk into a half-smile. He's actually not too bad... for a cat.

Walking past him, I head to the bottom of my steps to pick up the paper. When I get back to the top of the steps, Mo is gone, but there's a brochure or something in the spot where he sat.

Strange, he must've been sitting on it. I pick it up and see it's a travel pamphlet for Peru. Interesting. I stick it under my arm along with my newspaper and head back inside.

I walk straight to the kitchen island, where I left my hot cup of coffee, and take a seat on one of the wooden barstools. Opening up the newspaper, I take my time reading it from cover to cover, like I do every morning. The small words are becoming more difficult to see, which means it's probably time for some new glasses.

It's not typical for me to be easily distracted, but I keep looking over the top of my newspaper at the brochure. Finally, I can't take it anymore and set the newspaper down and pick up the brochure.

It's a tri-fold pamphlet detailing the Salkantay Trail to Machu Picchu. The brochure has colorful photos showing off the glorious views of the mountains and Machu Picchu itself. It looks like the travel company even sets up tents every night of the four-day hike.

This kind of trip wouldn't usually be something to spark my interest, but a part of me is fascinated. I love history. However, the idea of staying in a hut and hiking fifteen miles a day doesn't really speak to me. The times I've traveled with my family, we've stayed in five-star hotels that include a hot tub and room service.

My bet with Brooks pops into my mind, as well as the look of shock that would be on his face if I were to go on this excursion. It would be extremely out of character for me, but would definitely win the bet and show him I'm not so predictable after all—at least, not when I don't want to be.

I laugh to myself and pull out my phone to look up the travel company.

Sunday afternoon, I head over to my parents' house for a family BBQ. Normally, I'd be mildly annoyed about it since we just saw each other two days ago. But I can't wait to see the look on Brooks' face when I tell him about my trip.

I pull up to my parents' large historical home that's only about ten minutes from my place and see everyone else has already arrived. Usually, I make it a point to be early, but today I wanted to increase my shock factor by being late.

Heading straight to the backyard, I type in the code to the wrought-iron gate and let myself in. My parents have an impressive backyard. A gardener has professionally landscaped and maintained it weekly. They use the space to host many events, but I prefer it as it is now… with just my family.

As I round the corner, I see everyone gathered on the patio surrounding the large outdoor table as I expected. They're all gawking at me, making a show of looking at their watches. Of course, I assumed they'd be dramatic—they always are—but I'm amused by the rigamarole, nonetheless.

My mother enforces a certain… dress code… to our family BBQs. She seems to think the president could waltz into her backyard at any moment and we should all be photo-ready. Most of us appease her to keep the peace, and glancing around the patio, I see that it looks like a Vineyard Vines catalog could be shot here. The guys are wearing polos and khaki pants and the ladies all have on flowy sundresses. My eyes land on Brooks last and I resist the urge to wrinkle my nose at his messy hair and backward ball cap.

Brooks is the baby and has always been able to get away with anything. Mom would make me or Madden remove our hats to come into her perfect backyard. But not her baby. It doesn't really bother us, though. Mom is overbearing enough without us having to be smothered with her affection the way Brooks is. There's a part of me that wonders if that's why he dates no one seriously... he knows Mom will hate anyone he brings home.

Slowly, I swagger my way over to join everyone on the patio. With my hands casually in my pockets, I'm the picture of cool and collected.

"David, did you realize you're... *late*?" Mom asks, genuinely shocked. Or maybe perturbed.

I smile and adjust my glasses. "Yeah, this is the new me. Super chill and unpredictable."

Brooks guffaws. "Wow, do you think you're going to win the bet by being fifteen minutes late to a family BBQ? I don't think so."

He runs a hand through his blonde waves to sweep them out of his eyes. He needs a haircut; he's looking like Justin Bieber from 2008.

"Actually, I'm only thirteen minutes late." I pretend to inspect my fingernails, huff on them, and wipe the non-existent dirt away from my freshly pressed blue polo.

I smirk, and Brooks narrows his eyes at me. "However, I do think I'll win the bet with *this*." I pull the Machu Picchu travel brochure out of the back pocket of my khakis and hold it up for everyone to see.

Sophie comes closer to get a better look. "Peru?"

"Yep, I'm leaving in ten days," I tell them before casually taking a seat at the table. During my research last night, I discovered there was one slot left for September and I know September is the prime month to visit... at least it is according to the Peru documentary I watched last month.

Brooks sits in one of the off-white lounge chairs near the table and stretches his arms before resting them behind his head. "I'll believe it when I see it."

My dad takes the pamphlet and peruses it with Mom looking over his shoulder. Dad clears his throat. "Uh, you realize this is an *outdoor* hiking and camping expedition, right?"

"Yes, Dad. It's six nights total, and only four of those are camping. *Anyone* can hike and camp for four days."

"But David," Mom places a hand on my shoulder as she speaks, "you've never even left the country before."

I shrug her hand off with a bump of my shoulder. "I'm a grown man. I'll manage," I say confidentially, although I have my own doubts about that.

My brother-in-law, Drew, raises an eyebrow. He's solid muscle and is looking at me like he doubts my capability. "How many miles will you hike each day?" he asks.

I shrug my shoulders. "Ten to fifteen miles a day."

"It won't be easy. But it's doable." He sighs. "You really should've trained for a few months before booking the trip, but I'd be happy to work out with you a few times before you leave, at least."

I purse my lips, knowing he's right. But I wanted to book the trip before I thought about it too much and changed my mind or chickened out. I wanted to rip off the proverbial band-aid.

"That's probably not a bad idea. Text me your schedule and we'll plan a few times to work out."

He grins, looking way too excited about the prospect.

Odette and Madden are standing behind me and Odette pats my shoulder. "I'm proud of you, David. I bet you'll have a great trip."

Madden ruffles my hair. I hate it when he does that. "I'm proud of you, too. Can't wait to hear all about it."

"What about work?" Dad asks. Of course, that'd be what he'd think of first, with his workaholic tendencies and all.

I shrug. "Perks of owning your own business. I can take a vacation whenever I want."

Dad doesn't look convinced. "You rescheduled clients at such a late notice?"

"Seeing as I've never taken a vacation—ever—they didn't mind me rescheduling this once."

My dad shakes his head. "Bad business practice, son."

Sophie's eyes shift between me and my dad. She giggles awkwardly and changes the subject, "I'm not sure what's more exciting... David going on a big trip... or Brooks not being able to date for four months."

Everyone laughs except Dad who is apparently still concerned about me taking off work for the first time in my life.

The family turns their attention to Brooks. He's still sitting in his chair, looking unconcerned. "As I said, I'll believe it when I see it."

The rest of my family laughs and continues their meal, but I see the lone drop of sweat slowly making its way down Brooks' forehead.

Monday morning begins just like any other, except I've begun packing for an international trip. I don't leave for nine more days, but I did an inventory of my closet, knowing I'd need to do some serious shopping today. I don't even have hiking shoes, or a backpack... or a water bottle.

I start my day by getting dressed in business casual attire. Working from home doesn't mean being sloppy, and I meet with a lot of my clients over video chat.

After freshly grinding the coffee beans and filling my French press with hot water, I pour the coffee grounds on top and let it set while I head outside to get my morning paper.

Perfect coffee can't be rushed.

As I walk outside to grab my paper, I notice Isabella's yard is... once again, out of control. The grass—if you can even call it that—is long and overgrown. The weeds are growing in between all the cracks in the path leading up to her front door. Even the ants noticed how little yard work she does, taking full advantage by building an ant hill complex along her fence. Her yard alone ruins the look of the entire neighborhood. Everyone else's yards are perfectly trimmed, but she can't seem to manage her own.

I can hear her awful yoga music coming from her backyard—you know, the music they play in a spa, with harps and birds and all that bullshit—so I know she's awake. I see Mo clawing at the front window like he's desperate to escape. Poor animal. Even the cat hates her music.

How can she relax when there's so much work to be done? I've asked her several times to keep her music down and her lawn trimmed, to no avail.

Having not inhaled any coffee yet, I'm not in the mood to deal with my neighbor. I decide instead to go back inside and blare my own music. I have a fantastic Bluetooth surround sound system installed, which makes listening to my favorite audiobooks and podcasts delightful. But today I get to use it for a little heavy metal.

I snicker to myself sardonically. I hate heavy metal. Honestly, does anyone actually enjoy heavy metal?

It'll be enough to interrupt her yoga. I make sure the patio speakers are on and turn the music up to its max volume. I'd watch for her reaction since our yards are close together, but I have work to do. Grabbing my noise-canceling headphones, I finish the coffee and pour myself a cup before sitting at the kitchen table and opening my laptop.

Enjoying a perfectly brewed cup of coffee in peace while working on budgets for my clients are a few of the simple pleasures in life.

My open kitchen and dining room have French doors that open up onto the patio, giving me a clear view of my backyard and patio from where I sit at the dining room table. I watch Isabella fling open the gate to my side of the fence and stomp into my yard and straight to my patio.

Well, that was fast. Honestly, she makes this too easy.

She stops in front of the French doors and makes eye contact with me. Her chocolate-brown eyes are wild with rage, and I have to hold back a grin. She's dressed in her yoga clothes, which is distracting. A white, cropped, sporty top with matching white yoga shorts. The white stands out against her skin, making her look even darker and more bronzed. She knocks on the glass with one fist, then crosses her arms and taps her foot impatiently.

Sliding my headphones down around my neck, I rise from my seat and walk over to the French doors. Calmly, I open the door, then glance down at my Apple watch. "Siri, remind me to get a lock for the gate in my backyard."

The voice on my watch responds that she'll remind me tomorrow and Isabella's glare deepens. "You think you're really funny, don't you?"

"Is there something you need?" I lean against the doorframe and try to look bored.

"I think you already know why I'm here."

Bringing my hand up to my chin, I furrow my brow in mock confusion. "Hmm, I can't think of a reason."

She glances up at the speakers connected to the pergola above my deck—the speakers that are blaring heavy metal music—then back at me again. "Funny, you struck me as more of a classical music person."

My mouth is tempted to quirk into a smile at her sass. She's not wrong; I *am* a classical music person. But I'm not letting her know that she's correct. "I guess you don't know me very well."

She sighs. "David, turn the music off."

"I'll turn it off when you mow your lawn."

Her hands go to her hips. "Are you kidding me right now? That's what this is about?"

"Your yard looks like a jungle. It's uncouth."

"*Uncouth*? Who even talks like that?" She rolls her eyes. "My dad is coming over to mow the lawn later today. So can you please turn off the music?"

The knowledge that big words irritate her inspires me to continue. "Marvelous. I truly hope he cuts the grass posthaste."

She huffs and spins on her heel to leave. I shut the door, chuckling to myself as I flick the music off. I shouldn't enjoy seeing that look of ire in her eyes, but I can't help it. I enjoy it. My spats with Isa are the only exciting moments in my life.

"Isa," I whisper to myself, testing the shortened version of her name. I always thought Isabella was too formal a name for such a wild, sassy little thing. But *Isa* suits her perfectly.

Chapter Four

Isabella

Monday evening, Papa comes over after he gets off work. This is probably the main reason why he wants to marry me off… so he can have a break from mowing my lawn and being my on-call handyman.

He shows no sign of annoyance as he walks up my narrow walkway and grins at me. "How's my Bella?"

I smile, noting he's already changed out of his work clothes and into worn jeans and an old t-shirt. "Pretty good. Thanks for coming over and mowing. I can never seem to get the mower started."

Walking toward the small shed in my backyard, Papa releases a sigh. "Why don't you just ask that guy next door to help you start it?"

I scoff. "David?? You obviously haven't met him… He's perfectly proper and well-manicured. I doubt he could start a mower."

Papa chuckles and opens the shed door. “Ah, one of those types.”

I smile sardonically to myself, thinking of all the yard ornaments I purchased today at thrift stores. As soon as the sun goes down, David’s pristine lawn is getting a fun makeover.

My father pulls the mower out of the dusty shed and I hold the door open for him. “Are you good here, Papa? I was going to get some work done inside.”

He raises his eyebrows. “Are you *still* working on the little blog?”

Holding back a sigh, I answer, “It’s a website, Papa. And I have over 200,000 subscribers.”

He nods. “It better not get in the way of your work at Abuela’s.”

“Yeah, I know.” I give him a tense smile, not wanting to get into this yet again. “I’ll bring you some lemonade in a half hour, okay?”

“Sounds good,” he answers, then starts the push mower effortlessly with one pull.

I wish I could do that.

Ten minutes later, I’m back on the sofa with my laptop, scheduling my usual Tuesday and Thursday posts to my website for the next few weeks. I like to have my articles and posts planned out in advance so they don't interfere with my schedule at Abuela’s. And I never know if I’ll have service when I’m traveling. I always have my phone and laptop with me, but they are mostly for photos and videos since I don’t want to spend money on an international phone plan.

As long as I can take pictures and make notes for my travel and entertainment website, *Isa's Itinerary,* I don't care too much about not having Wi-Fi.

Mama and Papa pay us decent enough for working at Abuela's, but I have to stay on a strict budget so I have enough money to travel.

Working at Abuela's just doesn't fulfill me; it isn't my passion. I want to travel the world and explore. Not stuck in Kansas working in a kitchen. Or married off to the next man my parents find for me.

I click on a tab that shows all of my sponsorships and make sure I have what I need for photos in Peru. One of my biggest sponsors is a company that makes women's athletic wear. My contract states I need to make two posts a week that include photos of their clothing. This will be easy on a hiking expedition. I have all my favorite matching athletic sets packed and can take lots of gorgeous photos wearing them in the Andes Mountains. Hopefully the group I'm traveling with doesn't think I'm a huge dork for all the photos I'll take... but these sponsorships are how I travel every few months, so it doesn't really matter what they think.

After confirming I've packed all my necessary sponsored items and secured posts for the next two weeks, I realize it's been over thirty minutes and I need to get Papa's lemonade.

As I'm walking outside with his beverage in hand, I notice the sun is setting. I smirk to myself as I look at the sky. Almost time to make over my neighbor's yard.

The next morning, I'm woken abruptly by a very loud knocking that seems to come from my front door. Mo hisses at the sound, arching his back dramatically.

"Oh, calm down. You're fine," I tell him.

Sliding out of bed, I step into my fluffy white slippers and glance at my reflection in my floor-length mirror. I'm wearing lavender shorts that are silky and short, along with a matching spaghetti strap top.

I shrug. If they wanted me dressed, they shouldn't bang on my door at nine o'clock in the morning. My body is used to staying up late at night and sleeping in—struggles of working at a restaurant.

I pad down the short hallway, through the living area, and to the front door. More obnoxious knocking comes from the other side. I fling the door open to find David standing there, his hand raised mid-knock.

For a split second, he looks down at my pajamas. His cheeks flush slightly and he stutters, "Um, oh. Uh, about time you answered."

He holds up a flamingo in the hand he wasn't using to pound on my door. His lips twist angrily as he looks from me, then back to the flamingo.

I shoot him my biggest grin. "Well, good morning to you, too."

He takes a deep breath. I think he's attempting to calm himself. "You know, some of us have eight o'clock clients coming to our homes for business meetings."

"Wow, that's early for a meeting. Are you a drug dealer?"

He closes his eyes and mutters a swear under his breath. "If you must know, I'm an accountant and financial advisor. Hence the sign on my front door that says, 'David Windell, CPA and financial advisor,'" he adds dryly, like I must be a moron not to have noticed the sign.

"Clients sometimes need to meet before they start their workday. Something you obviously know nothing about."

I prickle at his jab. He doesn't know how hard I work, not only at the restaurant but also writing for Isa's Itinerary. I straighten my posture, trying to let his comment roll off me.

"The meetings are at your house?" I cross my arms and lift an eyebrow in question.

"I have worked from home since starting my business," he grits out.

"How does any of this have to do with you practically banging my door down at the crack of dawn?"

"The crack of dawn?! It's NINE." He shakes his head and groans. "This was my biggest client, and he thought he had the wrong house when he saw my yard covered in gnomes, flamingos, and cement geese."

I roll my lips together to keep from laughing. "Again, what does this have to do with me?"

"Even if I can't prove it, I know you did this." He thrusts the flamingo into my arms and turns to stomp off. "And why are the geese wearing weird little outfits? Infuriating woman." He waves his hand around in the air while he rants.

Before I can shut the door, Mo runs out the door and follows David back to his house.

I whisper, "Traitor." Like he can hear me.

I rush inside Abuela's a few hours later. I'm running late for my shift. I'm never late, but I got distracted finalizing things for my trip—and watching David from my window as he removed all the yard ornaments. The geese really weren't that heavy. He should workout more.

Internally, I'm praying my parents didn't notice I'm ten minutes late for my shift. I tiptoe into the break room and quietly sign in on the iPad system, then put my bag in my locker.

As I'm attempting to sneak past Papa's office, I hear him clear his throat from inside. "Bella."

I sigh in defeat and walk into his office. My father's office is simple, with white walls and a large oak desk in the center. Filing cabinets line one side, with a large screen displaying the security camera footage on the opposite wall. Mama has hung several family photos around the space, including old photos of the restaurant. One is a black-and-white photo showing my grandparents when they were young. My abuelito died a few months after it was taken. Mama is in Abuela's arms in the photo. She must have been about two years old. Next to it is a photo taken in the same spot, but it's of my parents in front of the restaurant with me and my sisters. This one was taken about five years ago. We took it a week after my abuela passed. Mama has since hung several more photos of Abuela around the room.

Unfortunately, both of my parents are seated like they've been waiting for me. Papa is seated in his large leather office chair, and Mama is resting against the edge of his desk.

"Wow, you both look twenty years younger today. Have you changed your skin care routines?"

"Nice try," Mama says, crossing her arms over her chest. "We've made it very clear to you and your sisters that our expectations for you are the same as every other employee."

"I know. I'm really sorry. I lost track of time getting everything ready for my trip," I admit. "It won't happen again."

Papa rubs his hand down his face. "I knew this ridiculous travel blog would distract you."

"I agree," Mama says, nodding her head. "You need to stop and focus on what's really important."

"What's really important?" I ask, grinding my teeth together.

"This isn't just a restaurant, Bella. It's a family tradition." Mama's voice is getting louder every time she speaks.

Papa gets up from his desk and walks over to close his office door. "Family comes first, and this is a *family* business."

"I shouldn't have to pour everything I have into this place to be a part of this family." My voice comes out louder than I wanted it to. I take a deep breath and close my eyes for a second to calm down.

"If our family was the most important thing to you, you'd be preparing to take over Abuela's someday, just like your father and I did." She points to the photo of our family on the wall.

"Why can't Rosa take over? Or Lily?" I rub my temples. "I love this family with all my heart. But restaurant management isn't my passion. Don't you want me to do something I love?"

"You're being selfish instead of setting an example for your younger sisters.You know your Abuela's lifelong wish was for you to run the restaurant someday." Mama stands and comes close so we're face to face. "Respect your Abuela's memory. And show your sisters that family stays together. They don't run off to different countries all the time and leave the work for everyone else."

Hot, angry tears fill my eyes. "We only have one life to live. I want to spend mine seeing the world, not being stuck in one place my entire life." Tears stream down my face. "My path doesn't have to look just like yours."

Papa pounds his fist on his desk, startling us both. His expression is one of anger and disappointment. "Enough! Bella, you will speak respectfully to your mother."

I meet his angry gaze with my own. "I'm late for my shift."

I exit the room and slam the door behind me, only to find my sisters right outside the door. They see my tears and both embrace me in a hug.

Lily speaks first. "They're too traditional for their own good."

Rosa smirks. "I'd love to take over the restaurant, so keep coming in late, by all means."

I laugh through my tears. "You two are the best. You know how much I love you, right?"

"Of course we do," Lily tells me while looping an arm around my shoulders. The three of us walk down the hallway toward the kitchen.

"And we love you too," Rosa says. "You should do what you're passionate about, what makes you feel alive. Mama and Papa will come around eventually."

"Maybe," I reply, trying to stay positive in front of my sisters. But deep down, I have serious doubts that Mama will ever be on board with me taking a different path than she did.

Abuela's death hit her really hard—it hit all of us really hard. Not only were we her only grandchildren, but we also worked together. And I know she wanted me and my sisters to run Abuela's together someday, but my grandmother also told us to do whatever made us excited to wake up every morning... only I think Mama conveniently forgot that part.

"I want to do right by our parents, but I can't keep putting my life on hold just to appease them."

Rosa sighs. "I know. We'll support you no matter what."

Lily loops an arm around my waist and leans her head on my shoulder. Rosa comes to my other side and links her arm through mine. The three of us walk toward the kitchen, connected to each other... literally and figuratively.

Chapter Five

David

I took my time plotting my revenge against Isa… Three days, to be exact. Ideally, she'll think I've forgotten all about the flamingos. But I haven't.

And I've concocted—heavy on the "cock"—the perfect retaliation.

I read through the ad I wrote for the wanted listings in the paper once more before submitting it online.

Wanted: Live roosters of all breeds and sizes. Wichita, Kansas, is in desperate need of a rooster rescue and I want to remedy that. If you have any unwanted roosters, please drop them off at the address listed below.

A chuckle rumbles out of my chest. It's a little higher-pitched than usual and I'm relieved no one is around to hear it. After paying the twenty-dollar fee for the ad, I hit submit and they send me a confirmation number and the date the ad will run, which is tomorrow morning. Friday will be perfect, seeing as she won't be able to call and dispute the ad all weekend since they'll be closed.

Having roosters next door will be annoying... but knowing how much she loves sleeping in, they'll annoy her way more than they will me. I'm up early, anyway.

There's a chance that no one will pay attention to the ad, but hopefully a few will be dropped off.

I can't wait.

Cleaning up the table from my rooster research, I pull up the link for my FaceTime meeting with a client who just started a non-profit in the form of a coffee shop. Helping entrepreneurs is my favorite part of this job. I love the challenge the larger companies bring, of course, but there's something about like-minded small-business owners that makes me love what I do.

I open the link and my client, Tom, pops up on the screen. He's a younger guy, probably mid-thirties, with red hair and green eyes. He's wearing a black t-shirt that has the logo of his new coffee shop on it.

"David! So glad we could meet so fast." He chuckles as he uses his hands to put air quotes around the word *meet*.

"You too, Tom. How are things going at Bean There, Roasted That?" I grin; it's impossible to say the name of his coffee shop with a straight face.

He ducks so I can see the view of the coffee bar behind him. "Great! Things are really taking off. But I'd feel better if I could get a grasp on these state non-profit taxes. You think you can give me some kind of estimate on how much to put aside once tax season rolls around?"

"I'll do my best." I pull up a new spreadsheet and get started.

That evening, I pull up to Drew's house—er, Drew *and* Sophie's house—for my first training session with my beast of a brother in law. Drew is waiting in the large garage gym he built with a big smile on his face. He looks way too excited for this, and that makes me dread it all the more.

But I like being prepared, and this is something I can do to make this Peruvian expedition more tolerable.

I park in the driveway behind Drew's Bronco and step out of my Land Cruiser. Drew meets me in the driveway but stops in his tracks as he takes in my clothing.

"What the hell are you wearing?"

I look down at my v-neck tee, linen shorts and leather loafers. "What's wrong with it? This is the most casual outfit I own... besides swim trunks."

He groans and motions with one of his muscular arms for me to follow him inside. "Come on, I'll let you borrow some gym shorts."

Reluctantly, I follow him inside, where my nieces attack me with love as soon as they see me.

"Uncle David!" Penny yells and runs to me before throwing her arms around my waist. I smile down at her and ruffle her dark-brown curls.

Samantha is never far behind her new big sister and hugs my legs. "Hey, Sammy girl," I say.

Sophie comes around the corner and giggles at the sight of the girls embracing me. "Hey, David."

Drew walks past her down the hallway toward their room and smacks my sister's butt as he passes her. She bites her bottom lip as she swats him away but he just chuckles as he disappears into their room.

"You guys are disgusting."

She looks slightly abashed and shrugs. "Newlyweds. Sorry."

Brooks bursts through the front door without even knocking. "Where are my two favorite girls?" he bellows.

Penny and Samantha run toward him giggling, and he picks both of them up in a big bear hug. When he sets them down, I notice he's wearing sneakers, red gym shorts, and a *Vote Madden Windell* t-shirt that he's cut the sleeves off of so you can see his arms and way too much of his armpits.

"Why are you here?" I ask. It's obvious he's here to work out, but he wasn't invited.

Drew reappears from the hallway and throws me a pair of black gym-shorts. "I saw Brooks at the store earlier and told him you were coming over to work out—"

"And I invited myself along. I couldn't miss out on the free entertainment," Brooks interrupts.

With a groan, I take the athletic shorts into the bathroom to change. The girls decorated the bathroom in a unicorn theme and the bathtub is filled with Barbies... and Barbie hair. Gross.

I slide off my linen shorts, then fold them neatly and set them on the bathroom counter. As soon as I step into Drew's gym shorts, I can tell they're going to be huge.

I sigh heavily when they slide right down my hips onto the tile floor. I yank them back up and roll the waistband twice so they'll stay up. Glancing in the mirror, I look lean and maybe a little pale since my skin rarely sees the light of day.

Smoothing my v-neck tee down, I decide I look decent enough and leave the bathroom. As soon as I step out into the main living area again, Brooks and Drew look me over. Brooks bursts out laughing and Drew pushes him.

"You don't have any tennis shoes?" Drew asks over Brooks' laughter.

I wrinkle my nose. "I purchased hiking boots the other day, but no tennis shoes."

Brooks walks up to me, still chuckling, and lifts my shirt. "Oh my gosh. You had to roll the waist band?"

"Shut up!" I shove his hands away and pull my shirt back into place.

Sophie looks at me sympathetically. "Don't let Brooks get to you. It's not your fault my husband is huge."

I look over at Drew, who is preening at her compliment. Wait, is he doing a Superman pose? What a weirdo.

"Can we please get this over with?" I ask before walking toward the door in the kitchen that leads to the garage.

As soon as I turn my back to the room, I hear Sophie reprimand Brooks and tell him to be nice to me. I withhold a laugh and continue walking until I'm in the garage. Drew and Brooks follow closely behind me.

Drew's three-car garage is large enough to store his precious Bronco, my sister's SUV, and one area completely dedicated to his gym. He's lined one wall with mirrors and the floor is covered in thick, black mats. On top of the mats there's a squat rack, a few benches, a long shelf for dumbbells, some kind of yellow and black contraption—I think he referred to it as a TRX band before—and some other machines that sort of look like black, metal praying mantises.

"Alright," Drew says before clapping once and then rubbing his palms together. "Let's get to work."

Brooks swaggers toward the weight rack and picks up a tiny pink dumbbell. It's obviously the smallest weight, as well as the only pink one. He hands it to me.

"Let's start you off with this one."

I glare at him. "Funny."

"Soph told you to be nice." Drew grabs the weight and sets it back on the weight rack. "Let's start with lunges, and then we'll do squats. You'll be using those gams while hiking, so we'll focus on that." He points to my legs, which compared to Drew's muscled calves look more like sticks than gams. "Grab the heaviest weights you can manage, and you can lower as you need to for each set."

I grab a fifteen pound weight in each hand and test their weight with a lunge. These feel good enough. I don't want to be so sore tomorrow that I can barely function. Drew grabs the fifty-pound weights and Brooks takes the forties.

Show-offs. At least *I* know what a bifurcated derivative is.

After completing our first set of lunges, Drew and Brooks both lose their shirts. Sophie brings out three glasses of ice water and Drew sneaks in a kiss. She pretends to be disgusted by how sweaty he is and I pretend to be annoyed by their public display of affection... but honestly, it's nice to see my sister so happy.

Brooks' phone rings in the middle of our second set. He grabs it out of his back pocket and smiles before answering. "Hey, Molls."

Molly is Brooks' best friend; they met at M.I.T. And now they co-own a medical supply company that they started after college. They specialize in plastic surgery, because of course Brooks would focus his skills on making people look better.

"They want to rush the order?" Brooks asks, his eyebrows drawing together briefly.

The muffled sound of Molly's reply goes on for a minute. I notice that Brooks' demeanor changes while he's on the phone. He's more serious, and even stands up a little straighter.

Brooks keeps his work life separate from his personal one. I never see him in work mode, but it makes me like him just a little bit more seeing him like this.

Brooks nods and then speaks into his phone. "Yeah, bring the contract by and I'll sign it real quick. I'll text you my brother-in-law's address." He smiles as she responds and then ends the call.

"Who are you giving my address to?" Drew asks in an annoyed tone.

Brooks grimaces. "Sorry, my business partner, Molly, is going to stop by so I can sign a contract real quick. She lives in this neighborhood."

Drew arches a brow. "You know someone in my neighborhood and you've never mentioned it before?"

He shrugs. "It never came up." His neck and face are growing more pink by the second.

I've always wondered if Brooks held a secret flame for his friend, but now my curiosity is piqued even more.

A sleek, white Tesla pulls into the driveway and Molly steps out with an iPad in hand. She's tiny and cute with thick brown hair and bangs. Molly is one of the few people I've seen that can actually pull off bangs. She's wearing a pink sundress and strappy heels that clack against the pavement as she walks toward us with a warm smile on her face.

Her step falters when she sees my shirtless brother. I don't miss the way she looks at him and how her cheeks turn the same pink color Brooks' were a moment ago. Brooks must have noted her discomfort because he walks back inside the garage and tosses his shirt back on.

She chuckles. "You caught me off guard, Brooks. I'm not used to seeing you so casual." Drew and I snicker at her comment. The only way we know Brooks is... casual.

Brooks shoots us a perturbed glance before turning his attention back to Molly, his smile firmly back in place. His posture is straight and he even runs a hand through his messy hair a few times like he's trying to look more professional in front of Molly.

He gives her a sweaty side hug. "You look great. Where are you off to?"

"I'm meeting Todd for dinner tonight," she answers.

Brooks' shoulders droop for a moment before he straightens his spine again. "Oh, fun. So I need to sign the contract for the new gluteal implants?"

"Yeah, sorry it's last minute." She unlocks the iPad and types in the passcode. "I printed off a hard copy for you, it's on your desk. But my contact for the plastic surgery center was adamant that the contract be signed as soon as possible."

"Got it." He leans over and takes the iPad from her and uses the Apple pen to sign the document she had pulled up. "Done."

"Thanks." She grins at him before looking over his shoulder at myself and Drew.

Brooks suddenly seems to remember we're here and turns around. "Oh sorry, this is my brother-in-law, Drew." He gestures toward Drew and she reaches forward and gives him a firm handshake. "And you've met my brother David a few times, right?"

"Nice meeting you, Drew. And David, good to see you again." She nods in my direction.

"You too. It's been a while."

An awkward moment passes before she speaks again. "Alright, well, I better head out. Todd hates it when I'm late."

I swear I hear Brooks swear under his breath. But I'm probably delirious from the physical exertion I've just been through.

"Have a good time. See you tomorrow," Brooks tells her with a strained smile.

Drew and I say our goodbyes and she waves before getting back in her Tesla and driving away.

"How have I never met your business partner?" Drew asks, the look on his face showing he's just as curious about Molly as I am.

"She's usually busy with her boyfriend," Brooks responds before ripping his shirt back off and walking back over toward the weights. He grabs Drew's fifties and starts lunging like a maniac.

"You don't like her boyfriend?" I push further.

He drops the weights abruptly. "The guy is awful. He strung her along all through college, and I've even seen him out with other women." He takes a deep breath. "I tried talking to her about him, but she just gets defensive and swears he's going to propose any day... but he never does."

Drew nods and grabs some weights. "You seem pretty passionate about the subject."

"Molly is my best friend. I don't want her to get hurt," Brooks says defensively. "Now let's get back to work."

Brooks starts lunging away from us and I give Drew a glance that says, *I have no idea what his problem is.*

Drew shrugs his shoulders and we start lunging again. Not even a half hour later, Brooks says he has to get home and go through the contract Molly dropped off. He's been unusually somber ever since she stopped by.

We watch his truck pull out of the driveway then turn back to each other. "What's up with him and Molly?" Drew asks the question we're both wondering.

I shrug. "You think he has a secret crush on her?"

"Definitely," he answers quickly, and we both laugh.

We finish our sets of lunges and Drew sets up the squat rack for me. The bar is forty-five pounds by itself, so I'm not sure why he's adding weights to it.

"So, how are you feeling about your trip? It's coming up."

I take a deep breath and then blow it out slowly. "Yeah, I leave in five days. Not gonna lie; I'm nervous."

Drew does one squat, instructing me how to use the proper form before responding. "You're a homebody, and there's nothing wrong with that. But I hope you can let loose and have a little fun."

Bending to get the bar onto my shoulders, I step back and start squatting. "Letting loose isn't my strong suit," I grit out as I pop back up and set the bar back on the rack.

"Four more," Drew says, pointing to the bar. "It'll be good to get out of your comfort zone; maybe you'll love it and start traveling all the time."

I glare at the bar like it has personally offended me, then get back underneath it for another squat. "Maybe. But I doubt it." I squat down and am breathing heavily. "I like...my own....mattress," I say with a groan as I force my legs back up and set the bar down once again.

Drew huffs out a laugh and then gives me an encouraging pat on the back. "You've never been camping though. Sleeping outside and being in nature... there's nothing like it, man. I love camping."

I'd roll my eyes if I had more energy. Drew goes camping all the time with his buddies from work.

"Oh, I almost forgot! I got you a birthday present. Be right back." Drew dashes inside the house, appearing a minute later with a Target bag. "Sorry I didn't wrap it."

He hands me the bag and I peek inside. There's a small black notebook with a stretchy band that holds the pages closed. "A notebook?"

Drew rubs the back of his neck like he's mildly embarrassed. "Yeah. When I turned thirty I started... journaling." His eyes become shiny like he's about to cry. "I'd write down my goals, my bucket list, my feelings." He clears his throat, which is apparently thick with emotion. "Sorry, you know I'm a crier."

"Uh, that's okay." Awkwardly, I lean forward and pat him on the back a few times. His very sweaty back. "Thanks for the present."

I set the bag to the side, and we continue our workout. By the time we've finished two more sets of squats, I'm wiped out and ready to go home. Drew tried to talk me into going for a short run... but I made an excuse about needing to get some work done. Thankfully, he bought it.

On my drive home, I wonder how I'm going to walk tomorrow... also what on earth I'm going to do with a journal?

Chapter Six

Isabella

I didn't bother setting my alarm for Friday morning since I closed at work the night before. I'm able to sleep in until about nine a.m., when I hear a rooster crowing. Deliriously, I throw my pillow over my head and fall back asleep. A few minutes later, I'm woken up again. This time it seems the roosters have multiplied. There's a lot of crowing going on, so it has to be more than one.

"What in the world..." I grumble to myself as I crawl out of bed.

Which one of my neighbors got roosters? It definitely wouldn't be David. He's no animal lover. I walk to my front door, still in my spaghetti strap nightgown, and peek out the front window.

My jaw drops and my eyes slowly widen when I see my small front porch is currently hosting half a dozen roosters. They're all in cages and look to be a mixture of colors and breeds.

"What the—" A knock on the door interrupts me mid-swear. I grab a zip up hoodie that's on my sofa and throw it on before opening the door.

Standing there is a short, older man dawning suspenders and a cowboy hat. He has a caged rooster in each hand. "Good morning, ma'am," he drawls in a thick Southern accent.

I can barely form words, but manage to stutter out a good morning.

"Saw yer ad, and brought these old boys by for your rooster rescue. Great work you're doing for roosters, by the way."

I blink rapidly. "I'm sorry, rooster rescue?"

He ignores my question and drops the cages on the porch, then turns to leave. "Have a good one!"

The two roosters stare at each other, then at me. I stare back at them, at a loss for words. I hear the man's pickup door shut and my brain finally starts functioning at full capacity.

I run toward him, waving my arms in the air. "Wait! Sir!"

He smiles and waves before driving away.

"This isn't a rooster rescue!" I yell, throwing my hands up. He's too far down the road for me to chase him, especially since I'm barefoot.

Standing there in the center of the street, I look from my front porch and then back to the man's truck, which is growing smaller in the distance. From the corner of my eye, I notice movement from David's front window and my head whips in that direction.

The curtains close abruptly, like he had just been holding them open and watching this entire scene take place.

"David," I whisper through gritted teeth. I should have known this was all him. He let the flamingo and cement geese debacle go too easily. Tip-toeing to his front door, I bang my fist on it as hard as I can.

A full minute passes, but I keep knocking. I know he's in there. Finally, he opens the door with a bored expression set firmly on his chiseled face. He adjusts his tortoise-shell glasses, which look new, and sighs.

"Can I help you? You're upsetting Mo."

I hear a little meow and look down at my neighbor's loafers. There he is in all his fluffy, traitorous glory.

"A rooster rescue?" I demand, using one hand to point toward my front porch. "Plastic animals are one thing, but live ones?"

"Plastic *and* cement animals."

I ball my hands into fists at my sides, trying to keep from smacking him in the face. "What am I supposed to do with eight roosters??"

He grimaces. "Nine."

"What?"

He nods his head toward my house and I look over to see an old woman dropping off an equally old-looking rooster. "No, no, no!" I run toward my house, stubbing my toe on a rock in the process. "Ouch!"

The woman sees me coming and waves to the rooster she's abandoning before running off down the street. Does she not own a vehicle? Where did she even come from??

"Ma'am! This isn't a rooster rescue!"

She cackles as she continues running away from me, remarkably fast for her age, I might add.

I can practically feel angry smoke coming out of my ears and nostrils, just like in those old cartoons. Slowly, for dramatic effect, I rotate my head to glare at David. "This. Means. War."

He smirks and then closes his front door, leaving Mo on his front door meowing.

After spending my entire weekend cleaning up chicken poop, finding homes for nine roosters, and working... I hardly had time to plan my revenge on my demented neighbor.

He thinks his clients seeing his yard filled with faux birds was embarrassing? Oh, it's about to get so much worse.

While cleaning up chicken poop from my yard and front porch on Friday, I heard him taking calls on his back patio. He probably thinks I felt humiliated with him watching me, but in reality I was making internal notes of all the appointments he set up for Monday morning.

I've been counting the minutes for Monday to finally arrive, and here it is.

Last night I hung David's new sign, which was previously a neat little plaque David hung on his front door during business hours. Well, his new and improved sign includes some much needed flare. His clients are sure to be impressed by his professionalism. They're also going to be wowed by his new business assistant.

With a peek at my watch, I see it's almost eight a.m.. I walk over to my floor-length mirror and straighten my tie. I'm wearing my most professional outfit: black heels, black trousers, and a white button up blouse, complete with a little black tie. I grab the stack of business cards I made at Kinkos and tiptoe over to David's front porch. Removing my heels, I carry them up the steps so the sound of my shoes won't alert him to my presence. Then slip them back onto my feet.

I smile at his new sign. It's fluorescent yellow poster board, the kind you'd use for an elementary school project, and covered with calculator stickers. His old sign was black and had the words *David Windell. Certified Public Accountant and Financial Advisor* engraved in gold lettering in a classic Times New Roman font. The new one has the same words, but I wrote them with my left hand so it would look extra messy. All the *I*'s have hearts instead of dots, which is pretty cute if I do say so myself.

But the business cards I made are probably what he'll hate the most. I had to really think of what would get to him, this man who's so dry and professional all the time... And then it came to me: Comic Sans font.

A shiny, black sports car pulls into the driveway and a wealthy-looking man steps out. You can practically smell the old-money wafting from him with his Ralph Lauren polo and freshly pressed dress pants. He's graying at the temples and has a fancy watch on his tanned arm.

"Good morning, sir," I say with a smile as he walks up the front porch steps.

One of his perfectly groomed eyebrows arches. "Good morning... I have a meeting with David Windell."

"Yes, Mr. Chamberlain, correct?" I remember that from eavesdropping the other day.

He nods, looking confused.

"I'm Mr. Windell's assistant, and due to food poisoning, he asked me to cancel his appointments today." I hand him one of the yellow business cards I'm holding. "Here's his card in case you lost his number."

He carefully takes the card, pinching it between his thumb and forefinger like it might be sticky. "Um, thank you. These are very... bright."

"I'll pass on the compliment. Mr. Windell is doing a branding overhaul."

Mr. Chamberlain grunts, then spins on his heel and walks back to his car. Once his car is gone, I pull my laptop out of the bag that I brought with me and schedule some articles to post while I'm on my trip—articles I meant to finish during the weekend before nine roosters appeared on my doorstep. At 8:45 on the dot, the next car pulls in the driveway.

"Jeez, these people are punctual," I whisper under my breath.

The next client's last name is either borington *or* lorington. It was hard to tell all the way from my front porch. David really needs to speak up when I'm trying to eavesdrop.

A middle-aged woman in a sleek pencil skirt and high-heels gets out of her SUV and walks toward the house. Her brown hair is in a smooth bob and she has glasses on that remind me of David's. She smiles warmly when she sees me on the front porch. Her eyes move toward the sign on the front door briefly and her eyebrows pinch together slightly before she turns back to me.

"Good morning Mrs. Blortington." I mix the b and l sounds together and hope she doesn't notice.

"Mrs. Lorington, yes."

Crap. She noticed. "I'm Mr. Windell's assistant. I'm so sorry for the last minute change, but Mr. Windell has food poisoning."

She gasps. "Oh no, the poor dear!"

"I know. He has barely left the bathroom all morning," I say, trying to look sympathetic about the illness I made up. "Here's his card to reschedule." I hand her one of the gaudy yellow business cards.

She eyes it and smirks. "Thanks, but I already have David's number. I've been friends with his mother for years."

"Oh, good." I huff out a sigh, trying to sound relieved. "He was too sick to forward me today's clients. So I'm just having to stand guard here and guess who's who."

"Right." She nods, but her eyes are squinting at me like she doesn't believe a word I'm saying.

Something inside of me is screaming, *abort, abort, abort! Mission canceled!*

Mrs. Lorington pulls a phone out of her briefcase and dials a number, then taps the screen to put it on speaker.

David's deep voice answers cheerfully—cheerfully for David, anyway. "Good morning, Mrs. Lorington, are we still on for today?"

She gives me a saccharine smile and her eyes are twinkling as if she's enjoying catching me in my lie. "I'm actually on your doorstep now, speaking with your lovely assistant. I'm so sorry to hear about the food poisoning."

He scoffs. "What? I don't have food poisoning, *or* an assistant."

David answers the door and I gulp the lump that's been stuck in my throat since she pulled her phone out.

He taps the screen to end the call, and looks between me and Mrs. Lorington before asking, "What are you doing here?"

I laugh awkwardly. "Just trying to help out, I know how busy you are with your clients."

"Mrs. Lorington, I'm so sorry about this." He touches her arm affectionately, like you would someone you've known since childhood.

She chuckles, looking curiously between the two of us. "Let's reschedule and I'll let you two take care of... whatever *this* is." She points from David then to me and back. She winks playfully at David before walking back to her SUV and driving away.

David crosses his arms and glares at me. I smile tightly at him and brace myself for a lecture. He looks me up and down, his eyes stopping on the yellow cards in my hand. He grabs my wrist firmly and pries my hand open.

He closes his eyes and runs his tongue over his front teeth before speaking. He's angry. Really angry. But I have to admire his self-control.

"Comic Sans?" He asks, finally opening his eyes again.

I bat my eyelashes innocently. "I thought your branding needed some updating... you know, to show how fun and silly you can be. Plus, they match your new sign."

His eyes widen and he turns around. He looks at the sign for about half a second before he rips it off and crumples it in his hand with a growl.

"Growling? Okay, now I'm scared," I say sarcastically. But when he whips around and pins me with those steely blue eyes... I actually am a little scared.

He uses his free hand to grab the yellow business cards from me. "Okay, we've had our fun with these... pranks," he says through gritted teeth. His self-controlled exterior slipping more by the second. "No more messing with my business."

I cross my arms. "And no more *live* animals."

"Fine." He narrows his eyes. "And by the way, no one would've believed your little charade this morning, anyway."

Mo makes an appearance on the front porch. I'm not sure if he came from David's house, or mine. I pick him up and hoist him over my shoulder before responding to David's comment. "Oh, really? Well, someone might want to inform Mr. Chamberlain, because he seemed pretty convinced."

Then I turn and walk back to my own house.

Chapter Seven

David

Two days after Isa's attempt to destroy my business, I fly to Peru.

I hardly slept last night, waking up over and over thinking I'd forgotten to pack my passport or something, just to get out of bed and check my bags for the millionth time. My knack for being prepared for anything came in handy for this last-minute trip since I already had an updated passport, despite having never traveled out of the country before.

Also, I'm still hot over Isabella's stunt the other day. Deep down, I know I asked for it with the roosters and all... but this is my business. Maintaining professionalism is of utmost importance to me. She has now made me look like a buffoon in front of clients, not once, but twice. Including the CEO of Wichita's largest construction company, and my mother's best friend who owns a successful cosmetics brand.

I started my finance business for the pleasure of working and the satisfaction of crunching numbers and helping businesses thrive. But between my trust fund and real estate investments, I don't *have* to work. If only my neighbor understood work ethic and responsibility. But she's too busy sleeping in until noon and doing yoga.

This trip couldn't have happened at a better time. I've never had a pressing urge to leave the comforts of home and country, but getting as far away from Isa as possible is pretty enticing. With each flight, my shoulders relaxed a little more, and I started enjoying myself just knowing I was getting further and further away from *her*.

When my last flight lands in Cusco, Peru, I get my suitcase and backpack from baggage claims and grab a shuttle to my hotel.

Checking into the hotel was no easy feat since foreign languages were never my strong suit. Our private school prided itself in teaching international languages… and despite taking Spanish and French all four years of high school, I still can't roll my *r*'s.

When I finally reach my hotel room, I feel slightly more at ease. I officially left the United States. With a deep breath, I tour the small room. It's nothing fancy, just a full-sized bed with simple white bedding, worn carpet, and large photos of Machu Picchu hung on the walls for decoration. I'll only be sleeping here tonight and the night after the expedition, so I didn't need anything extravagant.

After camping in the mountains for several nights, I'll probably need a vacation. A *real* vacation.

I take a shower then make sure my hiking backpack is packed and ready for the expedition—the hotel stores the rest of our luggage for us—then I pull back the covers and slide into bed. I should be exhausted after traveling all day, not to mention it's almost midnight, but stress is creeping its way back in. My thoughts are whirling again and my body is tense.

Before I completely spiral, I shoot a text to my family group chat.

David: Hey, wanted to let you all know I made it to Cusco City. Won't have service for the next five days.

Mom: So glad you made it safely!

Dad: Me too. Have a great trip and take pictures for us.

Sophie: And bring home a woman!

Madden: Forget a girl, bring home an alpaca!

Dad: An alpaca would be infinitely easier to care for than a woman... and cheaper.

Mom: Not funny.

Brooks: Don't think the alpaca would get along with your cat.

David: I DO NOT HAVE A CAT.

Brooks: Riiiiiiiiight. *wink emoji* I bet you miss him already.

David: *Eye Roll emoji*

David: Maybe I'll bring a woman home for Brooks... oh wait... he can't date for four months.

Brooks: *gif of a man crying and eating ice cream*

I snicker to myself and grab my phone charger. My phone pings with a text from Drew.

Drew: Heard you made it to Peru! How ya doing?

I take a deep breath and then release it slowly.

David: Anxious about tomorrow. I'm worried I'll miss my bus ride or forget something important.

Drew: Try not to overthink it. Everything will be fine. Can't wait to hear all about it when you get back.

David: Thanks, man.

Drew: Let's resume training when you get back, mmk? *gif of Spongebob lifting a stick with stuffed animals on each end*

David: *gif of Jim from The Office leaning the seat of Dwight's car back until he disappears*

Drew: Haha. Night!

I silence my phone, plug it into the charger, then turn my bedside lamp off. As I lay in the dark, trying to fall asleep, I swear I hear a woman on the other side of the wall who sounds just like my next-door neighbor.

Wow, I must be so exhausted I'm hallucinating. I realize I've gone this entire day without hearing a meowing cat, having an argument with Isa, or stumbling over a ceramic goose dressed in a rain jacket.

I smile to myself, relieved that at least I don't have to deal with any of that for the next five days.

Chapter Eight

Isabella

I'm finally in Peru, embarking on a journey I've dreamt of for years. I could hardly sleep last night I was so excited to start hiking and exploring. In four days, I'll finally see Machu Picchu in person instead of on my television screen.

I was a ball of energy during the short bus ride from the hotel to the meeting place for our expedition. When we arrive at our meeting place, I see that the porters already have the mules loaded up with everything the team needs to make camp each night. They're piled high with supplies, and I make a mental note to give the mules extra pets every evening.

Our group is easy to spot, not only because of the mules, but because all of the travel expedition employees are wearing matching green, long-sleeved tees with the travel company logo on the front. Their first names are printed on the backs of their shirts along with a little cartoon llama and fun letters that say, *Only you can prevent drama.*

We all pile into a small hut for a safety briefing. They announce that there are thirty-one people hiking in this group and then they go over some basic safety tips for the trek.

I already made friends with a young couple on the bus ride here from the hotel—perks of being an extrovert. I find a place next to Anthony and Hannah—aka my new besties. They're probably around my age, but they're both extremely fit and look like this hike will be nothing to them. Anthony has dark hair pulled back into a man bun, and Hannah is blonde with gorgeous blue eyes that remind me of someone's, but I can't put my finger on who. Definitely not David's.

Once our guides introduce themselves and their team, the safety briefing wraps up and we chat amongst ourselves for a few minutes.

Rocco, a native to the area and the expedition leader, whistles to draw the group's attention. "We have about fifteen miles to cover today, so let's get started!"

The group cheers and we begin our hike up the Andes.

About five minutes into the hike, Hannah strikes up a conversation. "So, Isabella, are you single? Because there's a really cute guy a few yards behind us."

"Hey!" Anthony says in mock defense. I note that he has a thick European accent, possibly Italian.

Hannah and I laugh. "Not nearly as cute as you, babe."

He winks at her.

"I *am* single. But I'm not looking for a relationship. My parents are already bugging the crap out of me about that." My breathing is beginning to get heavier as the incline becomes steeper.

I had hoped the extra strength training I've added in with my yoga would help me out, but I can already tell this trek will be a challenge.

"Ugh, parents can be so smothering sometimes," Hannah says, her voice not even strained like this is literally a walk in the park.

She glances behind her and smirks at me. "But… what happens in the Andes stays in the Andes… so no harm in a vacation fling."

Anthony scoffs. "Would you leave the poor girl alone?"

I laugh and Hannah joins me. Curiosity gets the better of me and I take a quick peek over my shoulder. My eyes widen and I stop dead in my tracks, causing a collision of hikers.

"David?!"

His bright blue eyes, a color that should look so friendly and inviting, meet mine. His eye color is a complete tease because they don't match his dark and dull personality at all. David uses his index finger to push his dark-rimmed glasses up his perfect, aristocratic nose and studies me for a second before his brain registers who he's looking at.

His eyebrows shoot up. "Isabella?" He closes his eyes and uses his thumb and forefinger to massage his temples as if my presence is causing him to have a brain aneurysm.

"What are you doing here?"

He huffs out a breath. "What am *I* doing here? What are *you* doing here?"

The rest of the group is making their way around us as we stand there, gawking at each other with annoyed expressions. Hannah and Anthony have stayed behind and are eyeing us with amusement.

"I booked this trip months ago. I'm 15% Incan and wanted to explore the land of my ancestors. I have every right to be here!" I raise my chin in defiance.

I'm not usually disagreeable, but this man brings out the worst in me.

"As far as I know, it's not a requirement to have Incan heritage to see Machu Picchu." His voice is calm and steady, as usual. If it wasn't for the twitch in his eye, I wouldn't even realize he was annoyed and not simply bored. "And besides, a brochure showed up on my doorstep."

I heave a heavy sigh. "That was probably *my* brochure."

"Is it my fault you can't keep your paperwork organized and contained within your own household?"

I'm grinding my teeth so hard that my jaw is starting to hurt. "Listen, Mr. Grumpy Pants," Hannah giggles and Anthony shushes her. "Let's just stay away from each other. There's no way I'm letting you ruin this trip for me."

"'Mr. Grumpy Pants'? Very mature." He clears his throat and begins walking to catch up with the rest of the group.

Anthony and Hannah start walking in the same direction, and I follow along. I take a few deep breaths and remind myself that I'm in a magnificent place, crossing a huge item off of my bucket list. I cannot let David drag me down.

I zip my fleece jacket up a little higher to protect my neck from the cold morning weather, and walk toward the group with determination in my steps.

An hour and a half into the hike, we stop at the gorgeous Humantay Lagoon. The lagoon's clear blue water is breathtaking paired with the snow-capped mountains in the background. We were all sure to dip our fingers into the freezing cold water since legend has it that the water keeps you young forever. I noticed David harrumphed when the guide told us that.

Does the man have no imagination?

Hannah was nice enough to assist me with photos for my website. Thankfully, she was already well-versed in iPhone photography and got a wide angle to show the entire lake but also capture my outfit spectacularly. My royal blue leggings and coordinating fleece jacket looked perfect next to the lake. My sponsors will love the photos.

After visiting the lagoon and taking photos, we continue our trek, still having many miles to cover today. During the hike, I'm able to observe the others in the group and notice everyone is paired up with a significant other, friends, or relatives. David and I seem to be the only ones solo on this expedition.

Oh well, I make friends easily—unlike Mr. Grumpy Pants who has kept to himself so far.

Seven miles in, we stop for a lunch break. The porters set up a tent for the chef who travels along with us and their team gets started with lunch prep. From my research, the food will be amazing.

I make sure to capture photos of the entire process before I take a seat on the ground next to a group of others, including Anthony and Hannah. I'm enjoying the view of the mountains and the cool breeze on my face. Just soaking it all in and allowing my legs to rest.

There's a group of four guys sitting in the circle next to us. I've chatted off and on with them today and they seem nice. They're childhood best friends and this is a trip for Eric, the one with shaggy red hair, who's getting married next month. Next to him sits Dustin, who's pale and freckled with blonde hair. The third one, Nick, has dark brown hair and hazel eyes. The one nearest to me is Chris. His hair is light brown and his eyes border somewhere between blue and green.

Eric, the one getting married, clears his throat. "So, Isabella, you're on this trip by yourself?" His eyes shift to Chris and then back to me. Chris begins to choke on the drink of water he just took from his water bottle.

"Uh, yeah." I shrug. "I tried to get my younger sisters to come, but they're not really outdoorsy."

"Ah, gotcha." He nods and looks at Chris again. "So, just curious... Who are you sharing a tent with tonight?"

Feeling creeped out by his question, I decide to be blunt. "Um, aren't you engaged?"

He chuckles and Dustin and Nick laugh along with him. "Oh yeah, I wasn't offering to share a tent. Don't worry."

Nick nudges Chris, whose face is bright red. "But this big hunk right here would be the perfect tent mate."

"There's not a more trustworthy guy," Dustin adds.

"Just something to consider if you don't want to sleep in a tent with some random weirdo," Eric says and the others nod in agreement.

I smile. "Thanks for the offer... but you're kind of all random weirdos at the moment."

Everyone laughs and Hannah joins our conversation, "I can share a tent with you. Don't worry about sharing with a creepy guy." She looks up at Nick and Chris. "No offense."

"But babe... it's our anniversary trip," Anthony reminds her, looking mildly annoyed at her offer.

"I know, but she's all by herself!"

"Don't worry about it." I cut in before Anthony can answer. "I'm sure I'll find someone to share with. Preferably a female."

Rocco, the expedition leader, announces lunch is ready and we all get up and make our way toward the tent. The food smells amazing, and we've all worked up an appetite. I glance around and notice David has been sitting alone several yards from the rest of the group. A very small part of me feels bad for him. Maybe if he wasn't so grouchy he'd make friends more easily.

Our group goes through the small buffet set up in a long tent and fill our plates with rice, fruit, and chicken. Then we shuffle to find our seats at the tables the porters set up for us. David is the last one out of the food tent and the only spot left is right across from me.

He glances at me, almost as if to ask my permission to sit there. I nod and he takes a seat, looking uncomfortable. His hair is in disarray from sweating and then getting blown around by the wind. He has a smudge of dirt on his shirt, which makes me smile. I've never seen him look unkempt and wild like this.

Chris is next to me; I'm noticing the guys in his group keep forcing us together whenever given the chance. Eric is seated across from us with David on one side, and Nick and Dustin on the other.

"How many miles do we have left today?" Chris asks his friends.

The three sitting across from us start counting on their fingers and looking up like they're internally calculating the math.

David glances at them, then calmly answers, "We've trekked seven miles so far, which means we have eight miles to go. Roughly twelve point eight kilometers."

He takes a bite of his rice and Eric stares at him with an annoyed expression.

"Dude, we can do simple math," Nick says defensively.

"I'm sure you can. I was merely answering his question."

Dustin leans over to get a better look at David. "Hey man, you forgot to take the tag off your fancy new backpack."

Eric, Nick, and Chris laugh at their friend's jab. Eric reaches over and yanks the price tag off of David's backpack. "Dude! Six-hundred dollars for a backpack?"

David shrugs, doing a fairly good job of pretending to be unfurled by their mocking, but his eyes are practically shooting lasers at them. "If I can afford the best, why not buy the best?"

Nick scoffs. "It's a hike, not a runway."

"You don't hike much, huh?" Chris asks him.

A blush creeps up David's neck, making his pale skin look red and splotchy. This is the first time I've seen him look so uncomfortable, perhaps even embarrassed.

"No, I don't hike much. I'm usually indoors... doing simple math."

He makes eye contact with me, and something about the look in his eyes and the guys making fun of him, makes me feel sympathetic to him being so out of his element here. I assumed he hadn't spent much time with the group today because he's a snob, but maybe it's because he's uncomfortable around people he doesn't know well.

I continue studying his features while the guys make jabs at David. The intensity in his expression conveys a vulnerability I haven't seen there before. His eyes are captivating by themselves but paired with his black-rimmed glasses, square jaw—complete with chin dimple—and mussed dark hair… he is a beautiful man. Infuriatingly so.

"Figures," Chris mutters under his breath. "If you got outdoors more often, maybe you'd get a tan."

Clearing my throat, I change the subject. Attempting to take the spotlight off of David. "Wow, this chicken is incredible!"

Chris stands with his empty plate in hand, then turns to me. "I completely agree! I'm getting some more food. Isabella, can I get you anything?"

Before I can answer, David speaks up. Apparently regaining his confidence. "Speaking of food, who's feeding Mo while we're away?"

The question draws everyone's attention back to David. Chris looks between us, his brow furrowed in confusion. "Who's Mo?"

I shoot David an annoyed look. Here I attempted to rescue him from their teasing and he basically announces to the group that we're neighbors.

"Mo is my cat," I answer without looking up at Chris. I keep my eyes narrowed on David. "And my sister is feeding him."

Without looking away from me, David replies, "Ah, I see. I'm glad I closed all my windows before I left the house. I tend to find him on my bed when I forget." The corner of his lips twitching just enough for me to know he's trying to get a rise out of me.

"Do you two… live together?" Chris asks, his voice cracking on the word *together*, like it pains him.

"No!" I answer, much louder than I intended to.

"We're neighbors. And unfortunately, her cat likes me better than her." David dabs his face with his neatly folded napkin.

Everything about his mannerisms makes it seem like he belongs at a fancy tea party and not a makeshift picnic area in the middle of the wilderness.

Chapter Nine

David

For the rest of the day, I try to stay close to Isa. I don't trust this Chris guy, and he hasn't left her side all day.

Jeez, Chris. Give the girl some space to breathe. If she wasn't so irritatingly gregarious, guys like Chris wouldn't be attached to her like a bee to honey.

She's being nice and friendly to him, the same way she is toward everyone else in our group, but she's definitely not being flirtatious. He just can't take a hint, and it's pissing me off.

I'm not jealous or anything, but as a man who has a sister, I feel the urge to protect. Her filling my yard with consignment store flamingos doesn't mean I want her to get murdered. Although that *would* make my life a little easier.

The fact is, you don't have to *like* someone to make sure they're safe. It's simply the right thing to do.

Mile after mile, it becomes more difficult to stay near Isa and Chris. I end up at the back of the group with the two oldest hikers, Gerald and Austin. They're identical twins and their constant jabs at each other are keeping me entertained.

And as much as I hate to admit it, being around the twins also makes me miss my own brothers. I can see how this trek would've been a lot more enjoyable had I brought them along.

"So, David, you keep staring at the lovely little gal with raven hair. Why don't you go talk to her?" Gerald asks as he adjusts his worn Booey hat over his white hair. "Shoot your shot, boy."

Austin nods his head in agreement. "You can't go five seconds without looking in her direction. Plus, that guy who's been on her heels all day seems like a twerp."

"Takes one to know one," Gerald teases.

I chuckle. "Isabella lives next door to me, and we don't exactly get along. I'm just trying to keep an eye out since she's traveling alone." I shrug. "I'd want someone to do the same if my sister was traveling by herself."

"Ahh, I see. So you're checking her out for her own safety then?" Austin winks and he and Gerald burst into laughter.

I shake my head at their antics but my lips curve into a grin. "You two are trouble."

"She's a pretty girl, David," Gerald says with a raise of his brows.

"Her looks are fine, but her personality?" I blow out a breath. "We'd drive each other to the brink of madness. We have nothing in common."

"Opposites attract." Austin grins, causing the wrinkles on his face to scrunch up. "Just like me and my Lale."

"Lale is, and always was, too good for you. She probably thought she was marrying me but just couldn't tell us apart."

Austin slugs his brother in the arm but Gerald just laughs.

My foot finds a loose rock on the path and I kick it to the side. "There are opposites… and there are mortal enemies. Big difference."

"There's a very fine line between love and hate, my boy," Gerald says and Austin nods in agreement.

We continue walking in amicable silence until we finally reach our campground for the day. Drew was right; I should've trained for weeks for this hike. I'm exhausted and ready for a shower and some sleep.

The porters have already set up our campsite when our group arrives. The mules are tied up to rest for the night. I feel sorry for them, doing this trek with supplies piled high on their backs. However, they don't seem bothered by it.

I remove my backpack and take a seat on the ground for a moment when movement catches my eye. Isa is near the mules and pulls something out of her jacket pocket. She pats each mule on the head and feeds them what looks to be apple slices from lunch.

I smile to myself as I watch her. She's quirky as hell, but there's something very endearing about her thoughtfulness at this moment.

Standing, I walk toward her. She notices me coming and wrinkles her nose in annoyance. This is the first chance I've had since early this morning to speak with her without Chris and his posse there.

I clear my throat, already regretting what I'm about to say. "I know we're not exactly friends–" I begin, but she interrupts me with a snort.

"That's an understatement."

I release a heavy sigh. "I overheard your conversation earlier about where you're going to sleep."

She crosses her arms over her ample chest and I shift my eyes to the mule next to me. "And?"

"Listen, you and I got off on the wrong foot from the moment you moved in next door and Mo invited himself over." I look down at my feet and kick a small pebble distractedly. "Maybe we can move forward? Instead of enemies, we could just be two people who don't really get along."

Isa stares at me with a befuddled expression.

"I, uh, wanted to let you know I can share a tent with you, if you'd prefer. The tents are decent in size, so we can have space. And at least you know *I'm* not a serial killer."

She raises one eyebrow. "Do I?"

I roll my eyes. "If I was, your cat would've been my first victim."

She surprises me by laughing. It's a rich, husky laugh and does something weird to my stomach. I haven't eaten much today, so that's probably the issue.

"Did Mr. Grumpy Pants just make a joke?" Her mouth curves into a wide grin, making me notice once more how soft and pouty her lips look.

"There you are!" Chris interrupts, walking toward us. "Dinner's ready." He glances at me like I'm an afterthought. "Oh, hey math guy."

"David," Isa reminds him.

"Huh?" Chris seems confused by her statement.

"My name is David," I answer on her behalf.

"Right." Chris places his hand on Isa's back possessively. "Let's go eat."

Isa steps to the side, putting some distance between herself and Chris, making me wonder if she's uncomfortable with his attention. She starts walking in the direction of the dinner tent and he follows on her heels.

This guy has no decorum whatsoever.

Isa glances over her shoulder at me. "You coming?"

The mule next to me nudges my side like he's encouraging me to go. He's probably not happy that I didn't bring him any apples.

After dinner, we take turns using the privacy screens to wash ourselves. Everyone is provided with a bucket of warm water to bathe with. It's nothing fancy, but it really felt good to wash up after hiking all day. I changed into some fleece-lined sweats and a red hoodie that says, *Madden Windell for Congress* on the front. Everyone on my brother's campaign team a few years back got one.

Our group huddles around a campfire after washing up and then hot chocolate is served. It's impressive how much thought and planning was put into this expedition.

I walk over to the table where they're serving the hot cocoa and grab a tin mug. The chef grins at me, and I thank him for the warm beverage before making my way to the campfire and taking a seat on the ground. My gaze instantly lands on Isa before anyone else, the soft glow of the fire making her brown skin look like it's glowing from the inside out. I'm not sure why I seem to seek her out today; maybe it's because she's the only person I know here, and I'm not very good with new people or building relationships.

If this trip has given me any epiphanies so far, it would be that I use my family as a crutch. As I've hiked throughout the day, I've realized this is the first time I've ever traveled without my family. I don't even hang out with anyone else. Even when I worked at an accounting firm before starting my own business, I never attended work functions.

Then when I'm home by myself every evening, I wonder why I'm alone. I'm pretty stupid for a smart person.

I realize Isa is posing with the fire in the background and the blonde girl, Hannah I think is her name, is snapping photos of her. Of all times to be taking photos for Instagram. I swear, women these days.

Isa meets my gaze, and I realize I've been staring at her. I quickly look down at my mug and take a sip of hot cocoa. I drink it too fast, not only burning my tongue in the process but making it go down the wrong pipe. I start coughing like a lifelong smoker and everyone stares at me with concerned expressions.

Our guide, Rocco, sits next to me and gives my back a few hard thumps. "You okay?"

I nod and he puts two fingers to his lips and whistles loudly to get everyone's attention. "Great first day everyone!" He claps for us and the group laughs softly. "So, we like to create sort of a family atmosphere on these expeditions, really get to know each other and make lasting memories. Why don't we go around the circle and tell everyone what made us decide to see Machu Picchu?"

Starting clockwise, everyone explains how they ended up here. Anthony and Hannah tell us they love hiking and this was one of the hikes on their bucket list, so they came for their anniversary. Chris and his buddies explain they wanted to do something unique for their friend's bachelor party. And Isa talks about her love for travel and wanting to see where her ancestors lived.

When everyone's finished, I'm the only one left. I shrug my shoulders and tell them, "I'm here because of a bet I made with my brother."

Isa's jaw drops open. "A *bet*?"

"Yeah." I grimace. "He didn't think I was capable of doing something unpredictable. So we bet on it."

Hannah, who's next to Isa, laughs. "Okay, we have to know what the bet was."

I run a hand through my hair nervously. I'm not usually one to speak in a large group like this. But everyone's eyes are focused on me, waiting for me to continue with my story.

Clearing my throat, I continue, "Basically, if I didn't do something unpredictable by Christmas, I had to go skydiving with him. But if I did... he couldn't date for four months."

Isa still looks shocked.

"So you already won the bet?" Hannah asks.

I grin. "Yep."

Chris scoffs. "Not going on a date for four months doesn't seem *that* crazy."

"Not for me either," I agree with him, probably the first and last time that will happen. "But Brooks is a serial dater. He can't go anywhere without flirting with a woman, or multiple women, and getting their numbers." Briefly, my mind wanders back to the awkwardness between him and Molly. I wonder if he's ever dated her?

Gerald and Austin guffaw from the left side of the circle. "Sounds like you back in your prime, Gerald!" Austin tells his brother, nudging his shoulder with his own.

Our group laughs and continues in conversation while we finish our hot chocolate. Rocco then stands up again and announces we should all get some sleep and rest for another day or hiking tomorrow.

Most everyone knows who they're sharing a tent with and grabs their backpacks, heading off to bed for the night. I stand and walk over near the tents, awaiting instructions from Rocco. Isa, Chris, and his buddy Nick, as well as Hannah and her husband Anthony, are standing nearby. I meander over their way as does Rocco.

"Isabella, it's really not a big deal for me to share a tent with you. Anthony will be fine." Hannah glances at her husband. His face is set into a serious pout.

"What's the trouble here?" Rocco asks.

Isa glances at me, raising her eyebrows slightly. I'm not sure if she's trying to silently ask if my offer to share a tent still stands, or if she's trying to convey that she hates my guts and wants me to fall off a cliff... so I just shrug my shoulders.

She huffs out a sigh. "Everything's fine. I'll be bunking with David."

"Are you sure you trust him?" Chris asks in a loud whisper.

She rolls her eyes. "Mo is an excellent judge of character; I'll be safe."

"Mo??" Chris asks, seemingly having forgotten our conversation at lunch.

"*Her cat,*" I remind him, feeling exasperated and ready to get away from him.

"I'm sure we can find a female for you to share with. It's very important to us that everyone feels safe here." Rocco looks intently at Isa as he speaks.

She smiles and places a hand on his arm. "Thank you, but I'm good. David and I are neighbors back home."

Rocco's shoulders relax. "Oh good, I didn't realize you two were friends before this."

Isa and I shoot each other a knowing glance, as if silently acknowledging that we're not friends, but we also won't murder each other. Well... I'm 99.9% sure we won't.

We all head off to our designated tents, Chris glaring at me over his shoulder before stomping off to spend the night with his friend Nick instead of Isa. I feel a sense of relief that she'll be with me—not because I enjoy her company, of course, but because I know she'll be safe.

I'm sure Chris isn't a bad guy or anything, but he's taken an obvious interest in her, and for some reason... it just doesn't sit right with me.

Chapter Ten

Isabella

David and I step inside the green tent, which is just large enough for two people, but with enough space that we don't have to be in each other's faces. We glance at each other awkwardly. We've never hung out, or even had a pleasant conversation. I inwardly cringe when I think back to our most recent interaction… which was me standing on his front porch, donning a tie, and untruthfully telling his clients he had food poisoning.

I was surprised when he offered to share a tent, but appreciative. Oddly enough, I do feel safe sharing a tent with him. Maybe because I met his sister and they seem like a close-knit family… so what he said made sense. Also, none of his pranks were necessarily dangerous or malicious.

If I'm being honest, the rooster thing was pretty ingenious.

Taking a seat on my comfy pallet, I unzip my backpack and grab my wool socks. While I slide them onto my feet to keep warm, I watch David from the corner of my eye. He's remaking the pallet that has been pre-assembled for us, folding the edge more neatly and layering the blankets in a different order.

"What are you doing?"

His head snaps up to look at me. "Remaking the bed for optimum warmth. Do you need assistance with yours?"

There's not a hint of sarcasm in his voice, so I can tell he's totally serious. I bite the insides of my cheeks to keep from smiling. "No thanks, I'll be okay."

I toss my backpack toward the end of my pallet, my deodorant and hairbrush falling out in the process but I ignore them and climb under the warm blankets. I take the hair tie from my wrist and lean back to shake out my hair before gathering the long locks into one hand and twisting them into a large bun on top of my head.

When I'm finished, I notice David silently staring at me from his now pristine pallet. "What?"

He looks away quickly, instead looking at my backpack and the items that are scattered beside it. He closes his eyes and takes a deep breath. "Isa, can you at least *try* not to make a mess?"

Isa? No one has ever called me that before, I wonder if he did it by mistake. Surely he doesn't know about my website. I used the name *Isa's Itinerary* to remain slightly mysterious, since everyone I know calls me either Isabella or Bella. Glancing over at his side of the tent, I notice his backpack is stowed at the foot of his pallet.

It's zipped and lined up perfectly with the blankets. He has what looks like a retainer case next to his pillow, and a tube of chapstick neatly lined up next to it.

Rolling my eyes, I reach for the items that fell out of my bag, shove them inside, and zip it up. I then throw it at the end of my pallet and cross my arms over my chest.

David purses his lips and we stare at each other for a moment. His eye is twitching again.

Finally, he breaks eye contact and leans over to grab my backpack. He shakes it out and sets it carefully at the end of my pallet so it looks just as tidy as his own.

He narrows his eyes at me before sliding into his pallet. "Don't make me regret this."

"Oh, brother." I snuggle down into my pallet.

David reaches for the retainer case next to him, opens it, and puts the retainer in, then makes himself comfy on his pillow and closes his eyes.

I can't help but heckle him. "Really? A retainer?"

His eyes snap open, making me once again notice the brilliant blue. Even in the dark tent lit only with a small lantern, you can tell his eyes are the color of Tahitian waters. "It's a nightguard. I grind my teeth at night."

He closes his eyes again, giving me a reprieve from their beauty. "I can't imagine why, seeing as you're such a pleasant and laid-back person."

He releases a heavy sigh. "It's been a long day; can we just turn off the lantern and go to sleep?"

"Fine," I concede. "Nighty night, neighbor." I flick off the light as he grumbles a goodnight.

I'm utterly exhausted from the trek today and know it won't take long to fall asleep. I close my eyes, feeling cozy under the thick blankets, despite the cold air. As I breathe in and out, I can't help but notice David's steady breathing and the smell of his skin filling the small space. It's a rich scent, like when you're walking through a fancy department store. There's no way he packed cologne for the trip; it has to be his natural scent. That rich and luxurious smell that's all his own.

As anticipated, I fell asleep quickly last night. I woke up with an ice-cold nose, but other than that I slept a solid six hours.

I roll over to see if David is awake, and to my surprise, he's still sound asleep. His neatly trimmed and usually well-coiffed dark hair is messy and sticking up in random places. One of his arms is thrown over his forehead and the other tucked beneath his blankets. Speaking of blankets, they're in complete disarray.

As if sensing someone is watching him, David startles awake, spluttering and sitting up straight. I giggle, unable to help myself.

"Whath's tho funny?" he demands, forgetting he has his nightguard in. He turns his head away from me and removes it before turning back around and putting it in its case. He clears his throat, "What's so funny?"

I sit up, dramatically looking over his messy pallet, and then back at mine, which is still perfectly intact since I'm a sound sleeper. "Why did you make such a fuss about your bed last night just for it to end up like that?" I gesture toward his pallet with my hand.

He brings his hands up and starts to smooth the covers. "It's not that bad."

"Not that bad? David, it looks like you did parkour in your dreams." I burst into laughter and he glares at me.

"I can't help how I sleep, Isa," He spits out before taking a deep calming breath. "I don't sleep well in strange places, okay?"

He called me Isa again. My heart does a little flutter at the endearment. It seems so uncharacteristic of him to give me a nickname, but I kind of like it nonetheless. "I'm sorry, I was just teasing."

He sighs. "Brooks teases me about it too."

"Do you and your brother not get along?"

He slumps back onto his pallet and stares up at the roof of the tent. "We do get along, in our own strange way. But our relationship mostly consists of roasting each other incessantly."

"I get that. I have two younger sisters."

He looks over at me and smirks. "I know. We're neighbors, remember?"

Of course he's noticed my sisters coming and going, the world's nosiest neighbor. "So you've been watching me?"

His cheeks turn pink. "Of course not," he says defensively. "It's impossible not to notice all the people in and out of your house. It's a zoo over there."

"Riiiiiiiight," I say in a teasing tone, throwing my covers off and grabbing my backpack. "Let's go get some breakfast, stalker."

I exit the tent and pull my shoes on. David follows closely behind me, looking irritated. He pulls his own tennis shoes on, muttering something under his breath about not being a stalker.

Anthony and Hannah are looking happy and refreshed as they walk by our tent. "Oh whew, you're both still alive," Hannah says with a smile.

Anthony smiles too. "Good morning!"

Chris, Nick, Eric, and Dustin are awake as well and are walking in the direction of the food tent. Something smells amazing, like bacon and eggs. The guys look up in my direction and smile, offering their hellos and good mornings. Except for Chris, who's apparently still pouting that I didn't want to share a tent with him. I literally just met the guy yesterday. Not only did I not want to sleep a foot away from him, but I also needed a break after he followed me around like a puppy dog all day.

Chris gives me a slight head nod in lieu of a good morning, then he glares behind me where David is standing.

Oh brother.

Chapter Eleven

David

After watching Chris pout all throughout breakfast, I was actually more than thrilled to start hiking again today. And that's saying a lot because my legs are pretty sore from yesterday's hike.

Despite having the naturally slender build that all the Windells seem to have inherited, my body isn't in great shape. And, unfortunately, working out with Drew twice didn't give me bulging muscles. My brothers always played sports and worked out, earning themselves well-defined physiques, but I simply never had the desire to exercise my body when I could be honing my mind instead. And if I'm being honest with myself, I was never naturally athletic the way they are. Academics always came easier to me than anything requiring hand-eye coordination.

However, I now see the perks of being physically fit. Working out with Drew on a regular basis is starting to sound like a good plan after all.

I stay toward the back of the group again today along with Austin and Gerald. We have a nice pace going that I'm comfortable with. My physical fitness might not be on par with Chris and Eric's, but at least I can convert miles into kilometers without using a calculator.

Imbeciles.

"So, how'd you sleep last night, Davey-boy?" Austin asks with a dramatic wink.

I keep my expression neutral. "Fine. Thank you for inquiring. How did you guys sleep?"

Gerald titters. "I told you he wouldn't give anything away. A gentleman never kisses and tells."

I shake my head. "And that's especially easy when there was no kissing to tell about."

"Well, maybe she'll warm up to you tonight," Gerald says.

Austin nods in agreement. "True, true. Women are like crockpots... takes em' a while to heat up."

I close my eyes, withholding a groan. "I'm not trying to warm her up. We're simply platonic tentmates for the next few nights."

Gerald holds his hands up in surrender. "Alright. If you say so."

Today is the warmest day of our expedition. It seems almost unnatural to watch the scenery change from glacial mountains and cold weather to a warm jungle atmosphere. I strip off my jacket and tie it around my waist, and notice most others doing the same. Isa removes her warm jacket to reveal a bright red sports bra, the same color as today's leggings. How many coordinating athletic outfits does the woman have?

She doesn't look indecent by any means, but I wish she'd put a shirt on... I don't like the way Chris is drooling all over her.

Begrudgingly, I look away from Isa and back to the mountain view. The view *almost* makes the hiking tolerable. I've never seen anything so majestic in my life; it's like everywhere you turn there's a scene so picturesque it could be in a movie.

Kansas, of course, is flat grasslands. Never would you round a corner and stumble upon a waterfall so grand it took your breath from your lungs. Nature has never been a great passion of mine, but I've found myself really enjoying the landscape here.

After four hours of hiking, we arrive at our campsite for the night. This campsite has showers, a pool, and even a hot tub. The group has all stripped down to the bare minimum of hiking clothes by now, and we all reek of sweat. Everyone seems excited to jump into the swimming pool and relax here for the evening.

All I want is a shower... a *real* shower. I've never smelled so bad in my life.

The ladies head toward their shower room, most of them planning just to change into their swimsuits. And the guys head to ours. We walk inside and see simple but clean cement floors and shower stalls. There are also bathroom stalls and sinks. It's no more than the average high school boys' locker room, but it feels like a luxury after two days of hiking.

The other guys change into their swim trunks while I go to a shower stall. I grab a bar of soap from my small toiletry bag and enjoy a warm shower and the scent of fresh soap. Once I finally smell like myself again, the place is empty except for me. I towel off and pull my swim trunks from my backpack and slip them on. They're simple, black swim shorts, but of course, the best quality.

Walking out of the shower room, I see our group at the pool. Everyone is splashing and having fun. I walk straight toward the hot tub, which is empty minus Austin and Gerald.

There's no way I'm getting into that pool; it's basically just swamp water now after all of those sweaty bodies have sloshed around in it. Gerald and Austin grin at me as I step into the hot tub and sink down into the bubbling water. It feels so good on my sore muscles and I instantly relax. Leaning my head back against the edge of the hot tub, I let my entire body relax and close my eyes... until I hear Isa shriek and then giggle.

My eyes snap open and my head jerks toward the sound. Anthony has Hannah on his shoulders, and Chris has Isa on his. They're playing chicken and laughing as they try to knock the other over into the water.

I swallow slowly as I take in Isa's hot pink bikini that shows off her amazing curves and gorgeous brown skin. Every inch of her body is perfect... soft curves, toned stomach, and long hair that falls down her back in a beautiful cascade of dark waves.

Gerald and Austin snicker, drawing me out of my Isa-induced stupor. My jaw, which I didn't realize was gaping open, snaps shut.

"You have it bad." Gerald shakes his head but has a teasing glint in his eye.

"So bad!" Austin agrees, and they both chuckle.

I clear my throat and sink down into the water. "Chicken might seem fun, but it's actually incredibly dangerous. What if one of them were to hit their head on the edge of the pool? I'm just concerned for everyone's well-being."

There's no way I'm admitting they're right... partially, anyway. I really do hate water games... but that's not why I can't take my eyes off of Isa. No, the cause of that is definitely the pink bikini.

Gerald and Austin glance at each other, then look at me. Both have their left eyebrows quirked, making them look even more alike than they already do. I ignore them and close my eyes again.

While my eyes are closed and I begin to relax again, I think about the mountain scenery, the waterfalls, the alpacas and wildlife we've seen, Brooks belching... *anything* but Isa in that little pink bikini.

After dinner, which consisted of grilled chicken, steamed rice, passion fruit, papayas, and oranges, everyone showers and heads to bed for the night. I assume I'm sharing a tent with Isa again tonight, but maybe she and Chris connected today and want to share.

My jaw clenches and I notice I'm grinding my teeth. I take a deep breath and crawl inside my designated tent. A few minutes later, Isa climbs inside as well. Wearing another sports bra, this one purple with matching athletic shorts.

"Oh, Isa, you're here," I declare the obvious like a total dumbass.

She looks at me with a confused expression as she sits on her pallet. "Yeah... is that okay? I thought we'd share a tent for the whole trip?"

"Right. Yes. I wasn't sure if you'd bunk with Chris tonight after your pool fun."

She smirks. "Am I detecting a hint of jealousy?"

I scoff and slide under my blankets, which are lighter and more breathable than the ones we used last night in the colder climate. "Don't be ridiculous. I hope the poor sap marries you, then I won't have to put up with you anymore."

She continues to stare at me with a twinkle of amusement in her eyes. "Then why were you watching us?"

"If you must know, pool games are extremely unsafe. I found it difficult to relax knowing someone might get hurt."

"Right." She pauses, still smirking. "You should've joined us. You were looking pretty good in those black swim trunks."

I blink rapidly, noting my face is suddenly hot. Turning away from her I pull the covers up over my bare chest. Since the weather is warm I opted to go shirtless.

She laughs and tugs on my blanket. "Don't be shy! Let me see that once-in-a-lifetime view of your exposed flesh. Which obviously hasn't seen sun... in a very, very long time."

I keep tight hold of the blanket, not because I'm self conscious, but because she's being an irritating ass. "Could you at least *attempt* to have some decorum?"

Isa squares her shoulders. "The woman has no decorum, shall we alert the queen??" she says in a deep voice with a horrible British accent.

"That was the worst British accent I've ever had the displeasure of hearing." I sit up to a sitting position and place a palm on her face to keep her an arm's length away.

She laughs and continues trying to swipe my blanket from me. We're facing each other now, both on our knees since the tent isn't that tall. My blanket is somehow still draped over one of my shoulders. She finally snatches it from me, and without thinking, I grab her hands and pin them behind her back, causing my arms to wrap around her in the process. Her big brown eyes, that suddenly remind me of those chocolate fountains people use at weddings, look up at me in surprise. Neither of us moves. Instead, we stare at each other. I wait a moment for her to wiggle out of my grasp, but she's perfectly still, her chest rising and falling slowly as she breathes. My brain obviously isn't working properly with her in my arms, since I then inhale the scent of her hair, which is down and still damp from her shower. The tendrils rest on my hands and arms and it smells incredible… like rose water and vanilla. Her lips look just as tempting up close, and her bronze complexion definitely isn't from makeup since she just got done bathing. She's somehow even more irresistible this way, natural and wild. Like a wild mustang that no one can tame.

Laughter comes from outside, causing our heads to snap in the direction of the sound and away from each other. I gulp, realizing how close we still are, and slowly release her hands.

She looks back up at me again and hands me my blanket. "Here you go."

I clear my throat. "Thanks… we should get some sleep. Night."

"Sweet dreams, David."

Chapter Twelve

Isabella

I awake the next morning with something warm and furry pressed along my torso and side. At first I wonder if David rolled over toward my pallet since he's such a crazy sleeper. Reaching my hand over my shoulder, I expect to feel human skin, or maybe chest hair? But my hand touches something *much* fuzzier than David, who has just the perfect amount of dark chest hair; nothing like the thick fur I feel against my fingertips.

I'm too groggy to put much thought into it, until I hear David's sleepy voice, "Oh, Isa, that feels nice."

He chuckles. It's deep and husky and laced with sleep. Is he talking in his sleep? I roll over and open my eyes to discover there's a large, furry, brown llama—or alpaca?—in between David and me. David's eyes are closed and he's smiling as the creature nibbles his neck and licks his hair.

"We can't do this now. Someone will hear," he mutters sleepily.

I bite my bottom lip to keep from laughing. Maybe my grouchy neighbor doesn't hate me as much as I thought he did? Whatever version of me he conjured up in his dreams seems to please him well enough.

As amused as I am, I'm also a little terrified that there's a wild animal in our tent. Llamas aren't carnivores, are they? I sure hope not.

I don't want to startle the poor thing, especially since she's so smitten with David.

I clear my throat, trying to wake David up. He stirs but doesn't open his eyes.

"David," I whisper.

He furrows his brow and pushes the llama's head away from his neck. "I said not now, Isa. Have some self-control."

I sit up slowly and shake my head. Does he really think I would just randomly start licking his neck? Who does that? Llamas... apparently.

"David," I whisper-yell.

He stirs again, his eyelids opening slowly then blinking a few times. He looks directly at the llama, and squints.

Right when I think he's going to freak out about the llama he's cuddled up with, he rubs his eyes with his fists and then leans onto his side, supporting his body weight with one elbow as he reaches for his glasses and slides them on.

His eyes widen and he just stares at the llama for a few seconds before squinting again. "Isabella?"

"This isn't *The Emperor's New Groove*, and I did *not* turn into a freaking llama!" I whisper-yell again and he finally notices me on the other side of the furry beast.

"So I'm assuming you weren't the one licking my face last night?"

I purse my lips and shoot him an exasperated look. "Nope. But you sure were enjoying your makeout sesh with your new llama-lover."

He furrows his eyebrows in a glare. "Don't even say that, it sounds weird." Apparently we're back to the grumpy persona again.

I roll my eyes. "How do we get her out of here?"

"How should I know?" he says through gritted teeth.

"You were the one moaning while she nibbled your earlobe. Figure it out!"

His jaw drops like he's offended. "I was *not* moaning!"

Our yelling spooks the llama in question and it stands up. The llama is much larger than I originally thought, and its head hits the top of the tent. The creature startles from the impact and spins in a circle. David gets on his feet, crouching down with his hands in front of him. It reminds me of Owen from *Jurassic World* working with the velociraptors. I'd laugh if I wasn't so terrified of getting trampled by the poor llama.

David glares at me from the opposite side of the tent. Crap... I think I said that *Jurassic World* thing out loud.

The llama attempts to run, looking for the exit, but not finding one. I shriek and cower into a corner of the tent, squeezing my eyes shut for a moment like that's going to make the llama disappear. When I open my eyes again, the tent is calm and the llama is nowhere in sight. David is standing by the entrance holding the tent flap open and looking very relieved. I'm still breathing heavily, traumatized by the whole thing and half expecting the fur ball to run back inside the tent.

David looks at me with concern. His blue eyes are soft and caring; possibly the first time I've seen them this way. He scoots toward me, letting the tent flap close behind him, then kneels in front of me.

"Are you okay?" he asks in a soothing voice. Then he places his hand on my arm, using his thumb to rub circles against my skin with a gentleness I never would have guessed he even possessed.

No, I'm not okay. Not when you're looking at me like that and wearing nothing but navy blue athletic shorts. "Yeah, I'm alright."

Rocco scares the bejeezus out of us both when he pops his head into our tent. "You guys okay in here? I heard screaming and then saw Lizzy fly out of here."

"Lizzy?" David asks dryly, obviously unamused by her name.

"Yeah, she's harmless, but she's a lot friendlier than the other llamas." He smirks. "Did you guys not zip your tent?"

David's head slowly turns to me and he has a murderous look in his eyes. So much for the soft gaze I got a few moments ago. *Sigh*.

"You were the last one in last night, Isa. Did you zip it?"

I grimace. "I can't remember."

He rubs his temples with his thumb and forefinger.

Rocco chuckles and informs us breakfast is ready.

Once he leaves, I try to smooth things over with David. "Listen, I'm sorry. It won't happen again."

He pulls on a t-shirt and socks. Which is unfortunate, because he has a great body. He's obviously not a meat head who spends hours at the gym, but there's something incredibly graceful about his lean physique and long limbs. He has that tall, slender build that wealthy families always seem to be blessed with. How do some people get all the good genetics?

"It's fine," he says. "Come on, we need coffee." He holds the tent flap open for me to walk through and then follows.

Throughout the day's hike, I stay toward the front of the pack with Anthony, Hannah, and Chris and his buddies, as usual. But I'm beginning to get a crick in my neck from looking back to see where David is at and who he's with.

As I take in the magnificent mountain views, I find myself wondering what David's reactions to the landscape are. Does his breath catch when he gazes out at the mountains? Does he smile at the wildlife?

I want to know it all.

There's something intriguing about the broody, handsome, accountant that I can't quite get out of my head. Especially after he looked at me so sweetly this morning when I was scared over llamapocalypse.

What would it be like to have the affection of a man who's so hard to win over? Someone who isn't even capable of useless flattery, but is always brutally honest to a fault?

"Wow, Isabella. The way you climb these rocks is impressive! You're in great shape," Chris tells me from a foot away.

I sigh, getting annoyed with his constant and ridiculous compliments. I'm *not* in that great of shape, and there's nothing special about the way I'm climbing these rocks. If David were up here with us, he'd probably explain what type of rocks they are and how many kilometers we have left to hike today. I smile to myself and glance over my shoulder once more.

This time, David meets my gaze and I smile at him. He looks serious, as usual, but one corner of his mouth turns up in a little smirk.

Hannah, who's beside me, clears her throat dramatically.

"What?" I ask.

She scoffs. "You know what."

I shrug. "Oh, stop. Our near-death experience this morning bonded us."

"I don't think having a llama in your tent constitutes a near-death experience," Anthony argues.

"Anthony's right."

"Thanks, babe," he says, giving her a smack on the bottom.

Hannah eyes Chris, who's a few paces ahead and lowers her voice to a whisper, "You *like* David. Just admit it."

With a groan, I admit, "I do not *like* him. But why does he have to be so handsome? That does make it a little more difficult to hate him."

She laughs. "Why do you need to hate him? He seems like a great guy. Smart, dependable, can defend you from evil llamas." She holds up a finger for each quality she lists.

"And he also smells really good... like insanely good. But what about how grouchy and serious he is?" I worry my bottom lip. "Back home we drive each other bonkers. You probably couldn't find two people more opposite than me and David."

"You might have more in common than you think. Try to get to know him." She stops and grabs her water bottle from her backpack and takes a long swig.

I rest my hands on my hips for a moment, feeling amused and a little annoyed by her comment. "You think David and I could have things in common?"

"Wouldn't hurt to find out," she says with a wink, then pockets her water bottle and jogs to catch up to her husband.

Instead of catching up with them, I purposefully slow my steps. Maybe it wouldn't be so bad to take it easier today. And if I end up hiking with David, then so be it.

Might as well have a positive relationship with my tent mate.

That night when I get done with my bucket bath for the night, I head to our tent to sleep. I think of my conversation with Hannah again. My mind has flitted back and forth about David all day, wondering if we actually do have similarities. Perhaps I've always focused on our differences instead of looking for things that might connect us.

When I slip inside the tent, David isn't inside yet. I place my backpack neatly at the end of my pallet, the way David does, hoping to start things off right tonight.

Rocco warned us there's a chance of rain tonight. I've always been scared of storms, which is stupid since I live in Tornado Alley. But I can handle some light rain. I dress warm in some grey leggings, thick socks, and a black long-sleeved, moisture-wicking top.

I hear the zipper to the tent and David steps inside after carefully taking his shoes off outside the tent first. He's dressed for a chilly night as well, with black sweats and a red hoodie.

He zips the tent door once he's inside and glances at my backpack stowed at the foot of my bed. He looks up at me through his dark eyelashes and smirks.

Pretending not to notice, I slide further down into my covers.

A light tapping sound fills our small tent and David looks up like he can see the sky. "I guess Rocco was correct about the rain."

I wrinkle my nose. "Yeah, I hope it doesn't get too bad."

He cocks his head to the side, looking at me curiously. "Are you afraid of storms?"

I scoff, and prop myself up on one elbow. "Of course not. I mean… they're not my favorite thing in the world, but scared? No way."

He looks unconvinced. "I didn't think anyone from Kansas was scared of storms."

"Like I said, I'm not scared—" I'm cut off by a loud crack of thunder. I throw the blankets over my head and cower beneath them.

David tugs at the blankets, but I keep a tight hold on them. The last thing I need right now is David's mockery.

"Hey, it's okay." His voice sounds... kind. And actually not mocking at all.

Hesitantly, I pull the covers back and peek at him. Thunder rumbles again, shaking the tent and making it feel like it's made of Saran Wrap.

He leans toward me to speak, like he doesn't want me to move from my cozy spot. "I researched the accommodations before booking this trip, and rest assured, these tents are very effective and structurally sound," he whispers to me in a soothing voice. The same voice he spoke with when the llama was trying to escape from our tent this morning.

If he's not careful, I'm going to grow accustomed to him being nice to me.

He continues to shock me when he moves to the other side of the tent and scoots his pallet right next to mine and crawls inside.

When he looks over and sees my surprise, he clears his throat. "Is this okay?"

I nod my head. It does make me feel less scared to have him closer.

"I, uh, used to be really scared of storms when I was little. I'd try to crawl in bed with my parents, but they'd tell me to be tough like my brothers and go back to bed."

Picturing a scared little David makes me want to wrap the man in a big hug. But he's opening up to me and I don't want to make any sudden movements and ruin it. "I'm sorry. My parents are all about tough love too. How'd you get over your fear?"

He smiles. "I didn't really, not until I was an adult. Instead, I started going to my older sister's room during storms. She'd lay blankets and pillows on the floor next to her bed and tell me stories until I fell asleep."

"Okay, that's the cutest thing I've ever heard."

He rolls his eyes, but he's still smiling. "My parents aren't all bad. They're just not very... sensitive. They have high expectations."

Wrinkling my nose, I admit, "Mine too. Especially Mama... she's more of a *'pull up your big girl panties and deal with it'* type of parent." I blow a breath out through my lips, making me feel like a deflating balloon. "My parents own a restaurant, actually. It was my grandmother's, and they took it over when she passed. They want me and my sisters to carry on the family tradition and run the restaurant once they retire... along with our husbands, of course." I roll my eyes then realize it's dark and he can't even see my eyeballs.

"Ahh, traditionalists. You and my sister would get along. Sophie and my parents really butted heads over the years."

"Yeah?" I look up at him with an arched eyebrow. "Did your parents want her to marry a Latin-American Catholic named Fabio?"

"That was oddly specific." His body shakes like he's trying to hold back his laughter, but he fails miserably and guffaws out loud.

I shake my head from side to side slowly. "You don't even wanna know."

"If your parents are anything like mine, they will give you some pushback in the beginning... but once they see you're happy on your own path, they'll come around and support you."

"You think so?" I ask, hoping maybe he's right and someday they'll come around.

"I really do. Hey, what restaurant do they own?"

"Abeula's Mexican Grill."

He huffs a breath out through his nose as if surprised. "You're kidding. I eat there with my brothers all the time. Abuela's has the best chimichangas in town."

"You should try the empanadas." I kiss my fingertips in a chef's kiss.

He breaks out in a genuine laugh, the deep sound making me feel warm inside. I realize then how cold I'm getting on the *outside*.

The wind picks up outside, whipping the rain against our tent. It's loud, but not as loud as the thunder. I scoot a little closer to David and he doesn't move away from me.

He continues the conversation, and I wonder if he's talking this much only to distract me from the storm.

"So, do you have a good relationship with your parents, or is it tumultuous?"

I contemplate for a moment before answering. "I love my parents, of course. They're just very traditional. In their minds, daughters should live with their parents until they get married at the age of twenty. Then their daughters will have children and everyone will spend their lives cooking Mexican food together happily ever after."

"I think our parents plan our lives out in their own minds, and when we do something completely different, they have a hard time letting go." He releases a heavy sigh. "With my parents, it's about money. As long as we're successful and make the Windell name look good, everything's okay."

I laugh, thinking about how posh David's family seemed when I met them briefly. "So, are you all really successful?"

I can hear the wrestling of blankets like he's fidgeting nervously and not wanting to answer. I click my tongue like a ticking clock, urging him to just answer the question already.

After a sigh, he admits, "My father is a surgeon, Madden is finishing up his second term in Congress, Brooks is a biomedical engineer, and Sophie's been forgiven for getting a teaching degree since she married a surgeon that works with my Dad."

"Wow, you guys really are just like the Cullens." I laugh and my teeth start to chatter from the chill in the air.

"The who?" David asks before lifting up his blankets and covering both of us with them. His blankets are warm from his body heat, and they smell like him, which instantly soothes me.

"The vampire family in *Twilight*."

His eyebrows pinch together in confusion. "Never heard of them."

I shake my head in dismay. "So, back to your sister, she did her own thing and your parents came around?"

"Yeah, it was a sore subject for a while... I think my Mom would still be thrilled if she quit her teaching job and hosted tea parties or something instead."

"I have some big dreams that are vastly different from my parents'," I admit. "So I think you're right; your sister and I would get along."

He brings a hand to his chest and gasps sarcastically. "I'm sorry, did you just say I was right?"

"Shut up."

"I wish I had a recording of that." He chuckles. "You'll have to tell me about those big dreams sometime."

I smile as a quiet moment passes between us. All I can hear is the steady drum of rain and the chattering of my teeth.

"Isa, I'm not trying to be a perv... but I think if you came closer to me you'd stay warmer. It's science."

"Oh, it's science, is it?" I mock, but I really am freezing my butt off. I can't even feel the tip of my nose anymore.

My teeth continue clattering away, but I don't move and neither does David... Until another burst of lighting lights up our entire tent. I jump and huddle against his warmth.

His chest is shaking and I'm not sure if it's because he's cold, or because he's laughing at me. But the heat from his body feels so good, I don't even care. I burrow my head into his soft hoodie and I feel the weight of his arm wrap around my shoulder.

Chapter Thirteen

David

Every time I think about waking up to a sleeping Isa this morning, with her soft hair brushing my cheek as she nestled her head against my neck, my stomach does this thing where it feels like it's doing a rendition of that scene from *The Princess Bride* where Wesley tumbles down the mountain and yells, "*As you wish*."

I'm exhausted today from staying up so late chatting, and Isa must be tired as well, because she's at the back of the pack with myself, Gerald, and Austin when she's usually upfront with the younger, fitness junkies.

I notice that the ornery twins fall back a few steps so me and Isa can walk side by side. The four of us are silently taking in the incredible view of the Andes Mountains, the peaks reaching so high in the sky that some are covered by clouds and fog. Everything surrounding us is so lush and green against the mountain backdrop that it feels like a dream.

Today we have a seven-mile hike before finally making it to Machu Picchu. We get to camp right next to it, which I'm actually rather excited about.

Rocco warned us we won't be able to see much tonight, as it will be extremely foggy until late morning tomorrow. But just knowing we made it to our destination will feel good.

This entire excursion has been eye-opening. I've never had the desire to explore nature and find myself... but I can see clearly how I've let my rigid routine and discomfort around new people hold me back from enjoying life. I thought enjoying life meant being comfortable, sleeping on my fancy mattress in my nice house, and having everything labeled so it's easy to access.

But I'm realizing that life is what happens when you get *out* of your comfort zone and really embrace the experience. The good, the bad, and the llamas.

This will definitely not be the end of my travels. My brain is swirling with other countries and ancient ruins I want to explore now, places I've only seen in documentaries. Much to my shock, getting out of your comfort zone is addicting.

"Hey, David?" Isa interrupts my thoughts, her voice sounding hesitant.

"Yeah?"

"This is going to sound weird, but would you take a few pictures for me?" she asks, drawing her bottom lip into her mouth nervously, like she feels uncomfortable asking.

"Um, okay. Right here?"

"I'll do a few different poses on that large rock," she points to the boulder a few feet from where we're standing. "If you tap the screen where I'm sitting, it will focus on me and blur the background."

"Alright, I think I can handle that."

She hands her phone to me and our fingers brush when I take it from her small hand, causing my heart to beat rapidly, just like it did last night when Isa jumped onto my pallet.

She clears her throat and walks over to the boulder where she gets into position for photos. She sits on it with one leg dangling and the other pulled into her chest. Today she's wearing a long-sleeved shirt and matching leggings in a brownish-red color, giving her gorgeous legs the illusion that they've been sculpted out of clay. I think I have a sudden interest in pottery.

I snap pictures with her phone as she does a few different poses on the rock. She even stands to do some kind of yoga pose.

She hops down and jaunts towards me. I hand her the phone and she scrolls through the photos. "These are perfect, thanks!"

"No problem." I shrug. "But I have to ask... what's with all the pictures?" We fall back in step, several yards behind Gerald and Austin now.

She scrunches her nose up before answering, "You promise not to laugh?"

"I won't laugh."

She takes a deep breath. "You know the big dreams I mentioned last night?"

I nod then look down at the ground and stick my hands in my pockets, hoping she doesn't notice the blush creeping up my neck at the thought of holding her last night.

"Well, I have a mildly successful travel blog. I go on trips every few months and document them with photos. I have a few sponsorships; one is from an activewear company." She gestures to her ensemble.

My eyes widen in surprise. *Wha— Isa? A travel blog? How—* My heart sinks. I had no idea my saucy little neighbor was an entrepreneur. I feel like such a jerk for assuming she just slept in every day and didn't have any drive. Didn't I make a comment to her face about being lazy? I cringe internally at the thought. No wonder she hates—er—*hated* me?

"That's pretty cool." I smile at her, and her shoulders relax like she was waiting for me to say something snarky... which makes me feel like an even bigger jerk.

I continue the conversation, genuinely interested in her travel blog. "So, what does *mildly* successful mean?"

"Well, I only have 200,000 followers. Ideally, to quit my day job, I'd need at least half a million to a million."

I try to school my features to contain my shock. Her blog isn't just mildly successful, it's *really* successful.

"Then I'd receive a lot more sponsorships and be able to travel more and have even better content."

I nod my head. "I must admit. I'm impressed."

She looks at me with a big smile, the small compliment obviously giving her a confidence boost.

I chuckle. "200,000 subscribers is amazing. I'd be happy to look over your business plan and give my input when we get back."

She looks over at me and narrows her eyes. "Is this just a ploy to get information so you can get your revenge for the Comic Sans business cards?"

A laugh rumbles out of me from deep down in my stomach, making me sound like my brothers when they laugh. Then the thought occurs to me... I've never laughed this much with anyone before now. I recall my conversation with Austin and Gerald about how there's a fine line between love and hate. And deep down, I know that line is already beginning to blur.

Chapter Fourteen

Isabella

If someone would've told me a week ago that I'd end up traveling to another country with my asshole neighbor... and enjoying myself.... I would've called them a liar. But spending time with David is surprisingly fun. Even the silences are comfortable and we have plenty to talk about.

Hannah was right; we're not as different as we thought we were.

"Do you like working from home?" I ask him, breaking the silence between us as we hike the last mile for today.

"I love it," he responds as he stops, removes his water bottle from his backpack, and takes a swig before continuing. "I'm my own boss and I make my own schedule. No more eighty-hour work weeks for me."

I sigh. "That sounds amazing. Do you travel a lot since you can work from anywhere?"

He scoffs before attaching his water bottle back onto his backpack. "Never. This is the first time I've ever left the United States."

My eyes widen at his admission. "You're kidding." He shakes his head, a look of sadness clouding his expression.

He continues, "I'm honestly shocked that I've enjoyed this trip so much. I'll definitely be adding several more trips into my schedule." The edge of his lips turns up into a smirk. "So I might need the URL for your website for ideas."

"Just google *Isa's Itinerary*." I bump his arm with my elbow playfully. "Hey, I've been wondering... Why do you call me Isa?"

His brow furrows as he thinks, then he opens his mouth to answer and closes it again.

I'm too focused on him to notice the loose rocks in front of me, and my foot slips. I shriek in terror as I fall towards the edge of the path with a steep drop-off. I have no idea how far the fall will be, but my guess is pretty damn far.

Right as I'm internally making peace with meeting my maker, David's hands grab onto my arms and pull me away from the ledge. For a moment, I keep my eyes squeezed shut and take deep breaths. When I finally pry them open, my face is buried in David's shirt. His scent, which is now familiar to me, envelopes my senses and calms me. David's arms are around me, one hand firmly on my waist and the other gently rubbing my back in a soothing rhythm.

I want to stay like this, wrapped in the safety of his arms, but our group is probably watching us and the longer he holds me, the more questions they're going to ask. I pull back and look up at David, his cool blue eyes laced with concern.

"Are you okay?"

I nod my head but keep my eyes locked on his.

He doesn't make a move to step away from me, instead keeping his arm around my waist.

We stand there with our gazes locked for what feels like a blissful eternity, before he finally breaks the silence. "I call you Isa," he says barely above a whisper, his chest heaving, probably from watching me nearly fall to my death, "because it feels right."

He steps back so there's an appropriate amount of space between us again. I glance over where we had almost caught up to our group and half of them are staring at us, the other half walking in our direction.

Rocco must notice the commotion and rushes over. "Everything okay?"

"Yeah, sorry. I stumbled on some rocks but I'm fine." I attempt a smile, but my whole body still feels shaky from nearly falling over a cliff, *and* from David's gaze nearly setting me on fire.

Hannah and Anthony break through the crowd. "Girl, your scream almost gave me a heart attack," Hannah says as she pulls me into a hug. She pulls away and grasps my shoulders to look me over, like she's making sure I'm not broken. Then she leans in and whispers, "thank goodness David was there to rescue you."

I blink to keep from crying, not wanting anyone to know how scared I really was, or how much I loved being rescued by David.

With a strained laugh, I shoo her away from me. "I'm fine, see? Not even a scratch."

Not even an hour after my near-death experience, we arrive at the edge of Machu Picchu where we'll camp for the night. Just like Rocco warned us, the thick fog is prohibiting our view, but hopefully it will clear in the morning and we can see the Incan ruins in all of their glory. The grass looks so thick and soft, I have the urge to lay down in it, and there's a large swing set so you can swing while taking in the Mountain Views.

The swing looks a little too close to the edge of the mountain for my comfort after my slip earlier.

Llamas are ambling about, grazing and seemingly oblivious to our arrival. They must be pretty used to tourists invading their turf. Llamas roam about here like cows in a pasture in the Midwest.

Hopefully none of them will try to make out with David tonight. I smile to myself as I remember that he thought I was the one doing that... and he wasn't trying to push me away. A shiver runs through my body, from my toes to the top of my head, making me feel warm and flushed all over.

What would it be like to kiss David? A man who's calculated and does everything with precision. Would that make him an excellent kisser, or a horrible one?

Someone clears their throat next to me, I was so deep in thought I hadn't even noticed them before now. I look over to see Hannah standing there watching me, one eyebrow quirked and a hand on her hip.

"With that glazed over look in your eyes and the blush on your cheeks, I'd think you might be thinking about a certain handsome accountant?"

I release a heavy sigh. "I don't know what's gotten into me. A week ago I couldn't stand him, and now I can't stop thinking about him? The altitude is messing with my brain."

She loops her arm through mine and directs us toward the tent where dinner is about to be served. "Like I said before, no harm in a vacation fling."

"Yeah, but David is the kind of man you settle down with... not the man you have a vacation fling with. And I have no desire to settle down and be chained to one city forever."

She scrunches her nose like she knows I'm right. "You have a wild soul, Isabella. But settling down isn't so bad when it's with the right person."

Anthony is waiting for her outside the dinner tent and they grin at each other as we get closer. "Maybe you need someone who will keep you safe while you keep them a little wild? I have an inkling that David needs a dose of wildness." She winks.

She lets go of my arm and heads into the tent with her husband. I stand there for a moment, contemplating what she said.

Could David learn to be a little wild?

Chapter Fifteen

David

I need some space from Isa. Her positive disposition and spandex outfits are doing something to my brain... like making me think I could tolerate spending time with her. Maybe hiking is giving me too much uninterrupted time with my thoughts... but I can't stop daydreaming about a future with Isa. My mind is conjuring up dreamy scenes of us traveling together, cooking empanadas in the kitchen... even having arguments about her messing up my alphabetized pantry system.

No one has ever gotten past my grouchy exterior the way she has. Isa has burrowed herself into my skin and made me want to open up and share everything with her. But I can't make sense of it. Why her?

I've had a lot of first dates. If Brooks is a serial-dater, I'm a serial *first*-dater. Because that's as far as I've ever gotten before my dates tell me they'll call me and I know they won't, but I don't really care because I wasn't into them either.

But Isa has me showing the side of myself that's witty and thoughtful, the side only those closest to me get to see. Not the side of me that's dull and folds my washcloths the same way, then makes sure they're all facing the same direction inside the linen closet.

I gave up years ago trying to find someone who could tolerate my cynical personality. Convinced myself I was better off being Uncle David… the guy who spoils his nieces and nephews and someday helps them with their algebra homework.

A few nights of sharing a tent with Isa and my brain has turned to mush. I enter the tent where dinner has been prepared for us. Gerald, Austin, and a few of the older couples in our group are seated at a table with one seat left. I quickly make my way over, knowing Isa will have to sit at a different table and maybe I'll regain all the brain cells I've obviously lost during this trek. I take a seat across from Gerald and Austin. Isa enters the tent just then and I meet her gaze across the tent for a second before making myself look away.

The twins wink at me, and I roll my eyes. If they're trying to be discreet, they're failing miserably.

Our table is full, so Isa takes a seat at the other end of the tent with the younger crowd. But she sits next to Chris and I feel my shoulders tense.

I drag my hands down my face, feeling frustrated with myself. Why should I be annoyed that she's sitting by Chris? She and I aren't together, and I have no claim on her. It's ridiculous that I've even developed the tiniest little crush on the woman... okay, maybe not *so* tiny.

I need a drink, and something stronger than this coffee we've been served. Although, I must admit, it's impeccable coffee. Harvested from a local coffee farm.

Tonight is my last night sharing a tent with Isa, and the realization makes my throat feel thick. Tomorrow night, I'll be back in my hotel room before heading home on an early flight the following morning.

All throughout dinner, I'm lost in my own thoughts and barely hear the conversations happening all around me. I manage to half-smile and nod a few times when spoken to so I appear mildly social. But thoughts of a certain raven-haired woman with enough spunk for five people is taking over all of my thoughts.

Spending the day with her was so effortless. The silences were comfortable, and the conversation was easy. I didn't even mind stopping to take photos for her every few miles. Especially now that I know she's a small business owner like myself. I admire people who work hard, and I was obviously wrong about Isa being lazy. She works full time at her parents' restaurant while also having a side hustle.

But where do we go from here? We've hated and pestered one another for nearly a year. If we can't get along as neighbors, what would a relationship look like?

And what makes me think she'd even want to go out with me? I'm probably reading the signs all wrong, like I always do with women. I wish women were more black and white. Easy to solve, like an equation.

Ugh, why didn't I pack that freaking journal Drew gave me? The one time I actually have enough feelings to write them down, and I didn't even bring it with me.

My head jerks up when a finger taps me on the shoulder. I look behind me and see Rocco standing there. The tent is now empty except for the two of us. I didn't even notice when everyone left.

"You okay?" Rocco asks, cocking his head to the side in curiosity.

I huff out a small laugh as I stand with my plate in hand. "Yeah, sorry. Just tired."

"No problem. Make sure you're staying hydrated." He smiles and gives me a pat on the back.

After putting my dishes away, I meet the rest of the group in front of the campfire. It's twilight now and the foggy haze makes the whole sky look rosy pink. The same color as Isa's pouty lips.

I grit my teeth and run a hand through my hair in frustration. "Get a hold of yourself, man," I whisper to myself.

Isa spots me walking toward the fire pit and waves me over, a big smile on her face. Great, now if I don't sit near her I'll look like an asshole. I force myself to smile and take a seat next to her in the circle.

Rocco comes over to the fire and gets everyone's attention by clapping his hands together once. He then goes into storytelling mode and tells us all about the ancient Incan constellations and the magic they were believed to impart. One of the other guides passes out pamphlets showing each constellation and where to find them in the sky.

I'm not usually one to believe anything that's not concrete and scientific, but if I can get along with Isabella Romero, this place must truly be magical. I listen raptly to Rocco talk about the stars in the wide open sky, right above this land where the Inca Empire once thrived, and about the magic they believed in... And for the first time, I want to believe in magic too.

By the time he's done pointing out each constellation and telling us the history behind it, I have goosebumps up and down my arms. It's definitely due to the magical constellations and not the fact that Isa's arm is brushing against mine.

Everyone disperses to clean up and get ready for bed. I draw out my time in the small bathing tent as long as possible, but there's only so much washing you can do with a bucket of warm water and a bar of soap, and I can't put off sleeping next to Isa any longer.

When I arrive at our tent, Isa isn't inside yet. I'm feeling antsy and decide to go look at the constellations myself, now that the fog has dissipated enough to see them. I pull out my constellation pamphlet and search for *Hanp' Atu: The Toad,* which is one of the constellations visible this time of year. Once I locate the Milky Way, The Toad isn't difficult to see.

"Are the stars showing you your path, David?" Isa's voice comes from behind me.

I turn and see her standing a few feet from where I'm sitting. She looks cozy in a white, fleece jacket and some simple black leggings. Her hair is up in a bun, but the wind has blown some loose tendrils down around her face.

"If only finding our path was that easy."

She sighs as she sits beside me near the edge of the mountain. "I wish it were."

"Me too," I admit. "Please don't fall, I'm too tired to save you again."

She punches my shoulder but laughs. We both sit for a moment, looking up at the black sky crowded with stars of all different shapes and sizes before she breaks the silence.

"You know, I had this grand idea that I'd feel a sense of belonging once I arrived at Machu Picchu." She looks down and plays with a blade of grass. "Like I was led here by some mystic power and would finally feel like I belonged."

I look at her in the light of the moon, and her sad expression makes my heart twist inside my chest. I know the feeling of not belonging all too well. "And you don't feel like you belong?"

She sighs. "No. But I'm not sure I'll ever feel that way..." She trails off, looking back up at the sky.

I don't often talk about my feelings, but Isa makes me want to open up and be vulnerable. To let her *know* me. And I have a strange feeling she'd understand me better than anyone else.

"I've often felt like I didn't belong. You've met my family," I huff out a laugh. "They're all athletic, charismatic... blonde." She laughs and I continue. "But... Have you ever wondered..." I pause, trying to think of the right words.

"Wondered what?" she asks, the light breeze blowing a damp curl across her face.

Without thinking, I reach over and sweep it away from her lovely face and behind her ear. "That a sense of belonging doesn't always come from a place, or even from your family... but maybe it only comes in the form of a person. That one person who just *gets* you."

She holds my gaze and I'm bewitched by the allure she doesn't realize she possesses. The enchantment of her positivity, her huge brown eyes that reflect the moonlit night, and her dark curls swaying with the wind.

She leans toward me, placing one small hand on my jaw and studies my face for a few seconds before leaning the rest of the way and pressing her lips to mine. I'm startled at first; I wasn't expecting her to kiss me. But with Isa, I never seem to know what to expect. I recover quickly and slide one hand into her thick hair, pulling her closer to me.

I haven't kissed a woman in a long time, and I haven't kissed many at all, but I'm 100% certain I've never had a kiss like this. And it's not because we're on top of a mountain overlooking Machu Picchu, or because we're hidden in the quiet darkness... It's her, this woman. I'm positive no one else could kiss me like this.

She moves her head to the side to get a better angle, and my control leaps out of my body and off the cliff in front of us. I pull her into my lap and slide an arm around her waist, the other hand still in her luscious hair, making her messy-bun even messier. She obviously doesn't mind because her arms go around my neck, drawing us closer together.

The croak of a very loud toad causes Isa to giggle and pull away from me slightly. Freaking toad, if I find the little bastard I'm gonna sacrifice him to the Incan Gods.

Isa smooths one hand over my cheek and across my jaw. "We better get some sleep."

With a sigh, I agree.

Chapter Sixteen

Isabella

It's confirmed. David can, in fact, kiss. That was the kind of kiss that makes a person settle down in Kansas forever, to build roots, have a family, live happily ever after.

Only, I don't want to settle down, remember? I'm not Cinderella. I'm Moana. Adventurer of the wind and sea. I will board my boat and travel the world. Figuratively, of course. I have no idea how to sail a boat.

Plus, my parents would never approve of David. He's not even Catholic… At least, I don't think he is. If I quit working at the restaurant to focus on Isa's Itinerary and start going out with a non-Catholic, they'll probably extricate me from the family entirely.

This is a harmless little vacation romance. What happens in the Andes stays in the Andes.

Our campsite is dark and quiet; David and I must be the only ones still awake. I slip into the tent and

David follows closely behind. We both slide under our blankets without a word. What does one say to their former nemesis that they just shared a passionate kiss with?

In the quiet stillness, I hear the shuffling of David's blankets and then feel his warm hand on my back. He gently massages my back and I smile to myself.

"Goodnight, David," I whisper.

"Night," he responds, continuing to rub my back.

I must have passed out quickly with David's soothing back massage, because next thing I know, it's morning. My stomach does a little flip when I realize today I'll finally get to see Machu Picchu. All of these miles we've put in will finally come to fruition, and we will see one of the seven man-made wonders of the world.

I sit up in bed and look over at David. He moved his pallet right next to mine last night and he's sleeping peacefully with one hand on his abdomen and the other across his eyes. His usual surly expression is now one of complete peace and relaxation. His hair is messy and his glasses are safely in their case beside him.

Smoothing one hand through his thick, dark hair, I whisper, "David, it's Machu Picchu day."

His eyebrows scrunch together but his eyes stay closed. I lean in and give him a quick kiss on the forehead. He hums contentedly, and a smirk passes over his lips.

"Lizzy Llama... is that you?" he asks, his voice raspy with sleep.

I laugh. "Sorry to disappoint... but it's just me."

He grins and opens his eyes. "Too bad. Lizzy was a really good kisser."

I lean back to rest on my knees and place my hands on my hips. "Better than me?"

He rolls his lips like he's really putting thought into the comparison between me and the llama. "Honestly, it's a toss up."

I lean forward and pinch his side, which makes him chuckle and twist up into a sitting position.

"Oh my, David is ticklish is he?" I continue pinching his sides in a tickling motion and he thrashes around like he can't control himself, laughing like I've never seen him laugh before.

"Stop, please stop." He grabs my hands and tugs me onto his lap like he did last night when we kissed.

He smiles and cups my chin in his hand and gives me the softest, sweetest kiss. "Good morning," he whispers against my lips, leaving me breathless.

David slides out from under me, grabs his glasses and puts them on. I notice he didn't put his nightguard in last night... which makes me wonder if he was hoping for more kisses. He starts packing his backpack up for the day and I sit and watch him. It's fascinating to me that he has a system for everything. He has small bags and containers within his backpack, so every item is labeled and has its own place.

What would it be like to be so organized? Does it make his life easier, or more difficult?

The pit of doubt in my gut wrenches once more. Because deep down I know this man isn't a vacation fling, he's the whole package... wedding, house, kids. I'm getting way ahead of myself here, but I can't picture my lifestyle of traveling and blogging meshing with David's at all.

As fun as the past few days have been with him, I can't change all my future plans based on like four nights in the same tent and a few stolen kisses.

As I pack my own backpack for the day, I remind myself. I'm Moana... not Cinderella.

When we exit our tent, we're greeted by the magnificent view of Machu Picchu in all of its glory.

The sight of the ancient civilization overwhelms me. My eyes fill with tears as I picture the Incan people building this and living their lives here. I imagine what it might've looked like filled with people. Families and their children, a market filled with fresh produce, animals ambling about. A grand city full of life and love. Maybe even the emperor and his guards at the top, overlooking the city.

These ancient ruins have stood through time. Their heavy stones carried by the Incans themselves, all the way up the mountains, then arranged in artistic patterns. How much work this must've taken... And what an honor to see it in person all these centuries later.

"Wow," David says, his voice cracking with emotion. "It's incredible."

Some of our group is already awake, taking in the same view. Others are just coming out of their tents and seeing it for the first time. Gasps and whispers surround us as everyone gets a view of the ancient relics for the first time.

Rocco walks up beside us. "Luckily, there's no fog today; sometimes people never get to see it in its entirety like this."

"Hiking all of those miles was definitely worth it," David tells him, making Rocco chuckle.

"I knew we'd turn you into a hiker," Rocco tells him with a slap on the back. "Breakfast is ready," he adds before walking off in the direction of the food tent.

David and I take one last look at the gorgeous view before following Rocco toward the breakfast tent.

Chapter Seventeen

David

It has to be the altitude.

What else could explain all of these feelings I'm having?

Actually, I'm not sure I've ever had more than one feeling at a time... but what I'm experiencing right now is an emotional overload.

Not only am I having deeply romantic feelings toward the same woman I loathed last week, but I had tears in my eyes looking upon ancient ruins... *and* I enjoyed this trip. I felt genuine happiness while hiking and camping.

I don't even know who I am anymore. Give me several equations at once and I will solve them so quickly people will look on in awe of my efficiency. But all of these emotions make my brain feel so full it might combust.

The breakfast tent is buzzing with energy and conversations about what their first thoughts were once they saw Machu Picchu this morning for the first time. Wonder and awe seem to be the general consensus.

Me and Isa are sitting at a table with the younger crowd. I normally sit with the older folks, but I can't seem to stay away from the real-life Incan goddess next to me. Well, 15% Incan goddess, anyway.

Despite the scent of breakfast and coffee filling the space, all my nose can focus on is the floral scent of Isa's hair that wafts my way everytime she moves. Today she's wearing leggings that are dark purple and a long-sleeved top that is a slightly lighter color and has a subtle floral pattern on it. The purple enhances her skin, giving her the appearance that she's glowing somehow, like her insides are made of sunshine.

Chris seems to have gotten over his infatuation with Isa and keeps to his man-friends. Eric talks about how he can't wait to get back to his fiancée tomorrow, and his friends tease him about taking his man-card away. Anthony and Hannah are already planning their next hike and discussing where they should go.

I withhold a grimace at the thought. I've definitely enjoyed this trip more than I ever thought I would, and it has inspired me to travel more and get out of my comfort zone. But excitedly planning my next *hike*? Yeah, I'm not quite there yet.

"You okay?" Isa asks in a hushed voice, probably noticing my pained expression.

I lean in close to her, so close my lips almost graze her ear. "I just can't imagine being so excited to hike again after this," I whisper.

When I pull away I notice the skin on her neck is covered in goosebumps, and I don't remember it being that way before. A thrill of satisfaction grows inside my chest knowing I can affect her in that way just with a whisper.

Is this what Brooks' life is like? But with every woman he comes across? I can see how it would get addictive holding that kind of power over the fairer sex. But the only woman I care to give goosebumps to is the one seated next to me.

Our group finishes breakfast in record speed, everyone anxious to go explore the ruins. Rocco leads us to a trail that takes us straight toward the ruins.

Isa asks me to stop and take some photos for her along the way, and I find that I'm getting pretty good at iPhone photography. I'll have to look up her website when I get home and see what she does with all of these pictures.

Once we arrive at the edge of the ruins, everyone disperses to explore, I stand back for a moment, not wanting to follow Isa around like Chris did. Isa gets a few steps away before she glances back at me over her shoulder.

"Come on, slow poke. You're my Instagram boyfriend for the day; who else is going to be my photographer?" She's teasing, but the word *boyfriend* causes my heart to miss a beat.

My thoughts drift once again to what that might look like. Would I sit around at home while she traveled? Would I go with her? Who would take care of Mo? Her parents are very traditional... Would they accept me, or convert me to Catholicism? I really hate the scent of frankincense.

Isa loops her arm through mine and basically drags me along beside her. I'm okay being dragged as long as I'm not following like a puppy. With every corner we turn, there's a new and breathtaking scene. The way the rocks are layered so precisely seems incredibly advanced for the time in which this ancient city was built. The craftsmanship is beautiful, and it continues down the steep side of the mountain.

I help Isa take photos in several spots and she even takes some of me. We come upon a group of llamas grazing at the edge of the ruins and she giggles and positions me in front of them for a photo. I stick my hands in the pockets of my black hiking pants and glare at her as she snaps photos, cracking herself up the entire time.

"Come on, smile! Your family will love this photo of you and your girlfriends." She grins and angles the phone for the perfect shot.

Her wide grin and messy hair make it impossible to remain stoic, and I find myself smiling in spite of myself.

She prances to my side and shows me one of the photos she took. I have a smirk on my face and three of the llamas even look up for the photo. "I'll send this one to you. I'm going to need your number."

I tilt my head to look at her and draw my eyebrows together like I'm really contemplating the idea. "My phone number? Are we ready for that step?"

She juts a hip out and pops her fist onto it in a sassy pose. "Seeing as we've already played tonsil hockey, I think we could exchange numbers." She smirks. "Plus, it would be so much easier to complain about your heavy metal music if I could just text you."

A deep laugh rumbles through my chest, surprising us both—and the llamas. "I'd almost forgotten about that."

She laughs. "So, do you actually listen to heavy metal?"

I pin her with an amused expression. "Do you really love yard ornaments?"

"Touché," She concedes. "You really are a classical music snob, aren't you?"

"Does having season tickets to the Wichita Orchestra make me a classical music snob?"

She scoffs. "Definitely."

I shrug my shoulders and we continue walking around the Incan ruins until we spot Anthony and Hannah. They're seated on the rocks, hand in hand, quietly taking in the scenery.

Isa rushes over and captures a picture of them. The faux camera shutter sound catches their attention.

"Oh, can you text me that one?" Hannah asks, standing up.

"I will!" Isa agrees and then sighs. "You guys are so cute."

Hannah reaches for Isa's phone, a smirk tugging at the corners of her mouth. "Okay, now let me get one of you two!"

Isa takes a few steps so she's right next to me and I slip my hand around her waist. We lean into each other and smile at the camera as if we've done this a million times. I'll definitely give Isa my number now, because I really want to hold onto that photo.

Hannah hands the phone back to Isa and she scrolls through the pictures, smiling at each one. I glance over her shoulder so I can see them too.

"Dang." Isa zooms in on our faces. "We look pretty good considering we've been hiking and camping for four days."

"You always look good," I say just loud enough for Isa to hear. She looks up at me with her chocolate brown eyes, and I take a second just to look at her.

"Hannah was telling me this would be a really cool spot for a wedding. Just in case you two needed any ideas." Anthony says with a smirk.

I huff out an awkward laugh and Isa rubs the back of her neck. Both of us are obviously feeling awkward at his assumption.

Hannah and Anthony laugh and Isa folds her arms over her chest and tries to look cross with them. "Hannah has you in on this now, huh?" she asks Anthony in a playful tone. "I told you two I have no interest in marriage... Too much of the world to see and too little time."

My jaw clenches at her statement, but I attempt to look unbothered. Does she really never want to get married? I mean, I know we've only kissed and talked about exchanging numbers, but what about someday... in the very, very distant future? Would she balk at the idea of marrying someone if she really loved them? Would she peg me as a traditionalist like her parents if *I* felt that way?

I've never entertained the idea of getting married, having never met anyone I liked enough to consider the idea. But I'd like to think if I fell in love, I'd marry that person and want a family with them. I see how happy Madden and Sophie are with their spouses and their adoration for their children, even though they're crazy, and I can picture myself having that—albeit with much better-behaved children... probably mathematical geniuses as well.

Anxiety makes its way throughout my body, causing a pit to form in my stomach. Me and Isa are so different. I take everything seriously and weigh my options carefully. Each decision I make I've put thought and planning into. If she sees no future with me and just kisses men on trips for the fun of it, then maybe this is better as a quick vacation romance. We can chock it up to the romantic scenery and magical Incan constellations, and continue as platonic neighbors once we arrive back home.

Chapter Eighteen

Isabella

After spending most of the day exploring Machu Picchu, we had the choice to hike the rest of the way down the mountain, about a three-hour trek, or purchase a ticket to ride down on the mountain train. I've enjoyed spending time with David so much, I'd assumed we'd hike down together. But David purchased a ticket for the train. He asked me if I wanted a ticket, but something about his body language made me say no. He seemed stiff and formal, like he did back in Kansas, before we'd kissed and shared a tent and looked at the stars. Before we developed feelings for each other.

Feelings that were real for me, but maybe weren't for him? Maybe he just needed some time alone. He seems like the kind of guy who'd need some time to decompress after a trip like this spent around people he doesn't know well.

I don't understand introverts.

About half of our group chose to hike down as opposed to taking the train, and by the time we make it to the bottom of the mountain, those who took the train have already taken a bus back to the hotel in Cusco City. I realize David and I never exchanged numbers and I don't even know which hotel room he's in. I really should've kept one of those ridiculous business cards I made for him.

As the rest of us wait for the next bus, I can't help but feel a little disappointed. And I hate that after this amazing trip, this is the feeling I'm left with. I force a smile on my face, hoping it'll make the rest of me feel better too, but it doesn't.

I sit by myself on the bus back to our hotel and make my way quickly to my room after grabbing the luggage they stored for me at the front desk. I'm tired from the trip and, oddly enough, I'm dreading sleeping alone tonight. I know David and I weren't *sleeping* together, but it was still comforting to have him there. Dependable, organized, steady David. He made me feel... secure, somehow. Like if my flaky brain forgot something or slept in too late, he'd have my back and keep me on track.

I've slept alone for twenty-eight years, but after four nights next to David, it seems pretty lonesome to do it again tonight.

On my way up to the room, I hope I might run into him and we can hang out or grab dinner, but I don't. When I make it to my hotel room, I fall face first into the mattress with a groan. I wish Mo was here; at least he'd keep me company.

Early the next morning, I pack up my belongings and head downstairs to check out and wait for the hotel shuttle to take me to the airport. The airline tickets were booked separately from our hiking excursion, so not everyone in our group has the same flights.

After I check out, I see a well-dressed man with perfect posture waiting in front of the hotel where the shuttles stop. I know it's David right away, not because of how amazing his butt looks in those khaki pants, but from the way he holds himself and how he keeps looking at the watch on his wrist. I smile and walk toward him. When he hears my footsteps and looks up, he smiles and my heartbeat starts salsa dancing inside my chest.

His hair is once again combed neatly with a little product to keep it in place. His dark glasses are polished, and he's back in his business casual attire complete with leather oxfords and a royal blue polo that brings out his brilliant eyes.

He looks good, *really* good. But a little part of me will miss the mussed hair, casual David that I got to see during our trek.

"Good morning."

He seems more relaxed today than he did last time I saw him, right before he boarded the mountain train.

"Good morning. You didn't miss me too much last night, did you?" He teases.

I bump his shoulder playfully with my own. "Please. I had so much room to sprawl out and sleep like a starfish. It was awesome," I lie, but say it in a sarcastic tone so he doesn't know how much I actually missed him.

He laughs. "What time does your flight leave?"

"10:45, Delta. You?"

"10:00, United." He sets the backpack he was holding next to his suitcase and sticks his hand in his pocket before pulling out what looks like a business card.

He hands it to me and our fingers brush when I take it from him. My breath hitches at the small contact, and goosebumps trickle down my arms.

Looking down, I study the card to steady myself. "Still using the boring business cards instead of the ones I made for you?"

"I shredded those. Comic Sans is an abomination," he says with conviction before the tiniest smile quirks the edge of his mouth. "My cell number is there. You know, for the llama photos you're going to send me." A shuttle pulls up in front of us, David grabs his luggage and hesitates for a second. "Well, I'll see you back in Kansas?"

I nod and tuck his business card into my purse. "See you in Kansas."

He opens the door of the shuttle that has the hotel's name on the side and gets inside. He waves before closing the door, and then the van drives away. I feel my eyes prickle with unwanted tears and I close my eyes to keep them at bay. When I open them again, I watch his shuttle until it disappears down the street.

"Isabella!" A voice calls from behind me, pulling me from my David-induced stupor. I turn and see Hannah and Anthony at the check out desk. I smile and head in their direction, not needing to leave for the airport quite yet.

Hannah meets me halfway and pulls me into a big hug. I lean into her embrace, feeling comforted after saying a strange goodbye to David and not knowing where we stand.

"I'm so glad we caught you before you left. I wanted to say goodbye," Hannah tells me, leaning back to look at me.

Anthony gives me a side hug. "Thanks for sharing a tent with David so I could sleep with my wife."

"Anthony!" Hannah smacks his shoulder, making him laugh.

"You're welcome. I got your back," I tell him. "I'm expecting a baby announcement by Christmas though."

I wink and Hannah squeals in delight. "Oh goodness, Anthony! Wouldn't that be a fun surprise! A little Machu Picchu baby!" Anthony puts an arm around his wife and pats her shoulder like he's trying to calm her down.

"I'm so glad we met during this trip," Hannah says, sombering instantly. "I wish we lived closer so we could hang out. But at least you have David." She smiles.

"Yeah, keep us posted on the David situation," Anthony grins.

My shoulders slump and I'm unable to act perky any longer at the constant reminders of David. "Yeah, I don't know. He didn't really act like he was interested."

Hannah and Anthony share a look with each other before bursting into laughter. "You're kidding, right?" Anthony asks.

"I don't know, I'm just confused. He started acting weird yesterday."

Hannah pats my shoulder. "Just talk to him. Maybe he's not sure where you stand either and where to go from here?"

I sigh. "You're right, I'll talk to him. I mean, we *are* neighbors. And he gave me his number."

"See?" Anthony says with a wave of his hand and I laugh.

The next shuttle pulls up outside and we say our goodbyes. I have Hannah's number so we can keep in touch, since she and Anthony live in Northern California.

Once my plane finally takes off, I feel anxious to get home. My stomach flips continually for the entire flight and I keep catching myself bumping my leg up and down nervously. I can't seem to hold still or ease my mind.

Maybe it would've been less awkward to just remain David's enemy… but now that I've experienced how funny and thoughtful he can be… I don't want to be his enemy.

When my plane lands in Texas for a layover, I shoot David a text before I lose my nerve.

I attach the photo of him glaring at me with the llamas in the background.

Isabella: Just in case you're missing your girlfriends, here's a photo for you to remember them by.

Three dots appear and then disappear several times before his response finally comes through.

David: There are definitely things I'm missing about Peru.

A few seconds later, he sends a picture of me curled up on my pallet, holding a blanket close to my face. I'm sound asleep. He must've taken it with his phone one morning before I woke up.

I grin at my phone, my heart fluttering with hope that this means he does feel something for me.

Chapter Nineteen

David

Pacing back and forth in my living room, I glance at my phone screen for the millionth time. I had just arrived home when Isa's text came through, and I got so pumped that she actually used my phone number that I completely lost my cool and sent a text that was obviously way too flirtatious because she never responded to it.

A knock comes from my front door before it opens, and Drew lets himself in.

"Welcome home!" He grins as he walks toward me, still wearing black scrubs from work. He must have just finished up for the day.

I continue pacing and his smile falters. "What's wrong?"

I tailspin into a summed-up version of the trip... not leaving out the fact that Isa ended up on the same trip, that we shared a tent, and how we kissed... several times. As he listens, Drew's facial expressions change from amused, to surprised, then... delighted?

Handing him my phone so he can read through our texts, I try to decipher his reaction as he reads, but he keeps his expression neutral.

I thrust my hands into my hair. "I must seem like the biggest creep taking photos of her while she was sleeping."

"David—" He starts, but I interrupt him.

"What was I thinking? I'm terrible at flirting. I have no idea how to portray interest without making myself appear to be a psychopathic stalker!" I throw my hands up in the air in defeat.

"Dude, chill." He hands my phone back to me. One of his eyebrows is arched like he might agree that I'm borderline psychopathic. "Is she even home from the airport yet? She probably hasn't even had time to respond."

I stop abruptly from my pacing. "You think so?"

"Yeah," he says before huffing out a laugh. "I've never seen you like this before. You're really into her."

I inhale a deep calming breath. "*No one* has seen me like this, because I never date. Because, obviously, I'm horrible at it."

Drew chuckles and takes a seat on my leather sofa, gesturing for me to do the same. "If I figured it out, so can you."

Taking a seat at the opposite end of my couch, I scoff at him. "Oh please. You're like a dark-haired Hercules with a doctorate. It's a miracle you stayed single for thirty-six years."

"Well, you have a point." He flexes his bicep, and pretends like he's going to kiss it. "Soph *has* told me I look like a Greek God."

My face twists into a cringe. "Ew, stop."

He throws his head back and laughs. "Alright, I want to hear more about your trip. You already told me about you and your neighbor sharing saliva—which honestly doesn't really surprise me—but how did you like camping?"

"What do you mean, it doesn't surprise you? It was certainly a shock to me."

He leans forward and rests his forearms on his knees. "Chemistry, David. You two have it. Simple as that."

"And you could see that from the few minutes we interacted at my birthday party?"

His lips curve up into a sly smile and he nods. "Soph and I talked about it on the way home that day."

I stare at him, feeling befuddled that others could clearly notice what I didn't. Drew cracks his knuckles then leans back into the sofa again.

"Did you enjoy the trip?"

Drew's calm demeanor eases my nerves, and I sink into the couch and relax a little. I'm glad he stopped by, even if it's just to distract me from the situation with Isa.

"I did, actually. It was... remarkable." I smile thinking of my days hiking with Gerald and Austin, the free-roaming llamas, and the delicious local coffee. "The experience definitely made me want to travel more." I chuckle. "And also start exercising regularly."

Drew pumps his fist into the air. "Yes! We begin training tomorrow."

I put my hands up, motioning for him to slow down. "Whoa there, I just got home. Give me a few days of R and R."

He reluctantly concedes. "Alright. But next week, you're coming over to work out with me."

Drew stays for over an hour while I show him the photos I took on my phone during my trip. I try my best to recount the details of the hike and what it was like to see Machu Picchu. I wish Isa had the post up on her website already; she'd probably be much better at giving the details people want to hear.

When I hear car doors closing outside, I nearly jump out of my seat. Drew stands and walks to the large window in my living room that has a clear view of my front yard and neighborhood.

He looks at me over his shoulder, his mouth spreading slowly into a wide grin. "Well, that's my cue to head home. Glad you're back."

We say our goodbyes and I walk him to the front door. After he leaves, I go back to the window so I can see Isa's house. It's dark outside now, but I can see the headlights of her car in her driveway. I release a deep breath, relieved she made it home safely.

My phone pings from where I left it on the sofa, causing me to jump. "Damn it, what's gotten into me? I've never been so jumpy in my life," I mutter to myself.

I walk over and grab my phone, smiling when I see it's a text from my neighbor.

Isa: Can't believe you took pictures of me when I was asleep. You're such a creep.

My heart plummets inside my chest for a moment, thinking she might be serious, until a photo comes through. It's a picture of me asleep with my shirt off, one arm slung over my eyes, and my mouth is open so you can see my mouth guard.

Drew was right and I was panicking over nothing. I laugh in spite of how ridiculous I look in the photo and text her back.

David: Never realized I looked so irresistible whilst asleep. No wonder Lizzy was so into me.

Isa: *gif of a llama blowing kisses*

The next morning, my alarm goes off as normal and I start my morning routine. Coffee in the French press, reading the paper, sneaking treats to Mo without anyone seeing… and glancing out the window at Isa's house.

Her yard obviously hasn't been mowed or maintained while she was in Peru. My yard guy came a few days ago, so my grass is freshly trimmed. There's even still a few of the chicken cages from last week strewn about on her front porch. But I'm partially to blame for that.

With a sigh, I sip my coffee and ponder for the hundredth time how she and I would ever work in the real world. In our everyday lives. Me with my schedule and an obsession with labeling everything... her with her travels and tendency to be... well, a hot mess. Emphasis on the *hot*.

Drew was right; we have chemistry. Amazing chemistry. But I'm not sure that's enough. I imagine that chemistry postpones most arguments in the beginning of relationships, when everything is new and exciting. But what about a year later when your significant other still throws their clothing *near* the hamper instead of inside the hamper? Or leaves their makeup scattered all over the bathroom counter? Or... puts cereal in the container labeled *Rice*.

I shudder at the thought.

Yeah, all of that chemistry that was so fun at the beginning will spontaneously combust and destroy the entire laboratory. And it won't be pretty.

Taking my mug of freshly brewed coffee to the table, I open my laptop and Google *Isa's Itinerary*. A photo of Isa in front of the Eiffel Tower pops up right away, along with a link to her website.

I click on the link and a pop-up appears, asking me to subscribe. Rolling my lips together, I narrow my eyes at the screen. I absolutely want to subscribe... but I don't want her to know I subscribed. I quickly type in my junk email address, which doesn't have my name in it, and click subscribe.

Her website fills my screen and I'm immediately impressed. I don't know if she designed it herself, but it's very professional. The tabs to skip ahead to different months are accessible and easy to find. And at the bottom of each article, everything she mentioned is linked on a website called Like To Know It. I'm assuming that's how she tracks people's purchases and gets commissions.

She even used an appropriate font. Arial. Solid choice.

I peruse her articles for nearly an hour when my phone pings with a text.

Isa: Found my website already, huh?

My eyes widen. How did she know?

David: Did you install a hidden camera inside my house?

Isa: Only you would have the email address: calc_u_later@wheatstate.net.

David: You got me.

Chapter Twenty

Isabella

Biting my bottom lip anxiously, I think of what to say next. I want to see him, and possibly get a better idea of his feelings. If he just wants to forget everything that transpired in Peru and be friends, that's fine.

Okay, it's not really fine. My feelings go way beyond friendship at this point and hopefully he feels the same way.

Isa: What are you doing tonight?

David: I have some work to catch up on. You?

Isa: Writing an article for my website on Machu Picchu and praying my neighbor doesn't interrupt my work with his heavy metal music.

David: Your neighbor sounds really cool and edgy.

Isa: He's alright. Do you think you'll be done with work by dinner?

David: Yeah, I should be.

Isa: Me too... So why don't we have dinner together?

I hold my breath and wait for his reply. My heart sinks when a whole minute has passed with no response.

A loud knock comes from my front door and my head snaps up. I walk quickly over to answer it and see David standing there wearing his signature outfit: a polo and dress pants. I look down at what I'm wearing: distressed shorts and the Abuela's Mexican Grill t-shirt I slept in last night. In my defense, I wasn't expecting him to come over.

"Are you asking me on a date?" he asks, crossing his arms over his chest. A smile tugs at his lips despite trying to remain serious.

"Yes. I am asking you on a date." I sigh and drag one hand through my hair. Oh gosh, my hair is still in the braided pigtails I did after my shower last night.

"Okay, but can I choose the restaurant?"

What an odd request. If he had a restaurant in mind, why didn't he ask me out? "Sure," I answer, then decide to mess with him. "But..."

His face falls. "But what?"

"Are you still seeing Lizzy, or did you end things with her?"

His shoulders drop as if relieved that I'm just messing with him. I burst into laughter at his expression.

David crosses his arms and pins me with a glare. I guess some things never change. "You're very easily entertained."

I meet his eyes and grin. "Lucky for you. That makes me a very low-maintenance date."

"You're ridiculous," He says, but can't hide his smile.

"How's six?"

"Sounds good. I'll pick you up here?"

"Okay. Oh, and please no Mexican food."

He chuckles. "Deal. See you tonight."

It took me most of the day to edit my photos from Peru and write a detailed article about the excursion. I included all the photos and details on how to book and what the experience was like. The words flowed from my fingers like never before; this is definitely my best article to date. Normally I only post articles twice a week, but I was too excited to wait and posted it right away. An email will alert my subscribers to a new post and hopefully it will have some comments in an hour or so.

I yawn and check the time on my computer, it's only three... that gives me time for a quick nap before I get ready for my date tonight. I don't normally have trouble sleeping, but last night and the night before were rough. Surely I didn't grow so accustomed to sleeping next to David that I'll be ruined for sleeping alone forever. I set an alarm on my phone and snuggle up on the couch.

An hour later, I wake up with my face covered in drool. Mo is on the coffee table staring at me. "What are you looking at? You drool all the time."

He turns his back to me. I stretch my limbs before grabbing my laptop to check my website. I'm anxious to see if anyone has commented on my new article.

Mo decides he's no longer disgusted by me and curls up next to me on the couch. I give him a scratch behind the ears and he purrs happily.

I pull up my website, and when I look at the number of website subscribers on the bar at the left-hand side of the screen, my jaw drops. I sit there stunned for several seconds before shaking my head like that will make the shock dissipate somehow.

Squeezing my eyes shut, I take a deep breath, then refresh the page. Surely this can't be right. I open my eyes and there it is again... 350,000 subscribers. Over a hundred thousand new subscribers since I posted my article an hour ago.

My shaky fingers scroll down to the bottom of my post to read the comments and I gasp, causing Mo to startle next to me. He gives me an annoyed look and moves away.

Over five thousand comments. I've never had this many. I average about two thousand comments on each post, which I thought was incredible, but this is a magnitude I never thought I'd reach. And it's only been an hour.

I scroll and begin to read through each comment, some telling me how gorgeous the photos are, several saying they purchased a few of the active wear sets I linked, and even more talking about how they now want to book a trip for themselves to see the ancient ruins.

Happy tears start to trickle down my cheeks until they speed up and I'm sitting on my sofa in a puddle of my own tears, completely overwhelmed by the success of this post and the positive commentary.

Wiping my face with the sleeve of my oversized t-shirt, I take a few calming breaths and open my email. Hundreds of new emails greet me and my eyes fly over the titles. Most of the emails are new sponsorship opportunities and companies wanting me to promote their products.

One email catches my attention and I click on it first. It's from the marketing director of Monaco Hotels Inc. Monaco Hotels are a major international hotel chain known for their five star restaurants and full-service spas.

I read and then reread the email again and again. Making sure this is actually real. They're offering me a paid sponsorship. The amount they'll pay me along with complimentary stays in their hotels would be more than enough for me to travel full time. This is the opportunity I've been dreaming of, I just never thought it would happen this soon.

I'm looking over the contract attached along with the contact info of Bridget Lecour, the marketing director. She wants to meet with me in person to go over the contract—*if* I'm interested.

OF COURSE I'M INTERESTED!

But there's a lot to consider here, namely the rift this will cause between me and my parents... but also this new thing sprouting between me and David. We haven't even been on our first real date and we'd have to do the long distance thing. It could never work.

I have some big decisions to make. My phone pings with a text, and I welcome the distraction from my thoughts.

David: Pretty sure I didn't give you permission to post that picture of my ass on your website. You'll be hearing from my lawyer.

I chuckle, feeling pretty flattered that he took the time to read my article so soon after I published it. I know just what photo he's speaking of. You can't see anyone's face, but David is in front of me as we're hiking and his backside does look pretty fine. I even got a few comments about it.

Isabella: Hm, are you sure it was yours? I thought that was Chris.

David: Chris's backpack wasn't nearly as nice as mine. I'm sure that's me.

Isabella: Oh, sorry about that. Several women in the comments would like the phone number of the owner of that ass. You want me to give it out?

David: No thanks. One woman driving me crazy is more than enough.

I grin down at my phone. After all this time, why did we have to start enjoying each other *now*? If we still despised each other it'd be much easier to leave.

Looking myself over in the floor length mirror in my room, I do a little spin to make sure I look alright. For how little time I had to get ready, I look pretty good. I'm wearing wedge espadrilles and an off-the-shoulder red dress that has layers of ruffles sewn on. I grab my denim jacket since it's September and it might get chilly once the sun sets. I put my hair up in a braided bun on top of my head with a few curls left out around my face and neck. My makeup is minimal, except for my red lipstick that matches my dress.

Glancing at the clock, I sigh in relief when I see it's ten til' six and I'm ready to go. David strikes me as someone who's always early, so I planned accordingly. As if my thoughts conjured him, a knock comes from my front door. I basically twirl my way to answer it, my tummy doing little flips like it's twirling too.

I open the door, unable to hide the excited smile on my face. David is standing there with a bouquet of red roses. Classic, like the man himself. He's dressed in a crisp white shirt, rolled up to his elbows, and tweed trousers paired with his oxford shoes. His glasses can't hide the sparkle in his blue eyes. There's something softer about his eyes now compared to the hard look they held before our trip to Peru. Like our trip together softened him up and turned them from ice-blue to the color of the Peruvian sky.

He drinks me in from my toes to the braided bun pinned on top of my head. His gaze heats up the longer he looks at me.

"You look like you're ready to go salsa dancing." His eyes stay heated with appreciation but one corner of his mouth pulls up into a smirk as hands me the roses.

"Thank you," I tell him, taking the roses and closing my eyes as I inhale their scent. "Come in for a sec while I put these in a vase." I move to the side so he can come in.

He pulls the door closed behind him and follows me as I walk into the kitchen and take a large vase out of the cabinet and fill it with water.

I glance over my shoulder and see Mo rubbing against David's legs. David reluctantly bends down and gives him a rough pat on the head. Mo doesn't seem to mind and leans into his caress.

Placing the vase that's now filled with water on the counter, I unwrap the flowers and put them into the water before walking back toward David and Mo.

"I like your place," David says, shoving his hands into his pockets as he looks around my small house. "It looks like you."

"Old and eclectic?" I wrinkle my nose and he laughs.

He brings a hand to his chin like he's concentrating on how to explain himself. "No, it's small and minimal, so you could pack up at any moment and take off on an adventure. But it has just enough of the things you've collected while traveling to make you feel a sense of home while you're here."

I blink a few times and swallow the lump in my throat. How he managed to sum it up so perfectly has me at a loss for words.

"Are you ready to go?" He pops his elbow out like he's escorting me to prom.

"Yes, I'm starving," I admit, taking his arm. "Bye, Mo, be a good boy."

We walk out the door together and I close it behind us. Mo claws at it from the other side.

"Poor beast. We'll bring him back some leftovers."

"David, are you warming up to my cat?" I bring my free hand to my chest, feigning surprise.

He ignores my comment.

Twenty minutes later, we pull up outside a steakhouse I've never been to. It looks fancy and the host knows David by name.

"Mr. Windell, we have your table ready," the boy tells him. He's probably not a boy, but he looks barely eighteen. He walks toward the back of the restaurant and we follow him.

David places a hand at the small of my back as we walk, the warmth of his hand sending a tremor of pleasure down my spine.

We walk through the restaurant. It's dark here, but in a romantic way. The walls are lined with stone like we're inside a castle and they're lit with lanterns. More lanterns adorn each table, giving the place an old-world feel. We walk past the bar, which is made of a large slab of distressed wood. The bartenders are dressed in white shirts and black suspenders, another nod to a time gone by. We walk past the bar and the main restaurant area, then down an arched hallway that recedes down as if we're going underground.

The host opens a wooden door and leads us into a large room with a huge stone fireplace. The ceiling is high and there's a large, rustic chandelier hanging from the center. Hunter-green armchairs rest in front of the fireplace and they look soft and luxurious, like velvet. A small round table has been set for two a few yards from the fireplace.

"Thank you, Johnny," David nods to our host as he exits the room, closing the large wooden door behind him. David gestures toward the table and pulls out the nearest chair, which is the same velvet as the arm chairs in front of the fireplace.

I take a seat, still in awe of the gorgeous space. "This is so cool. It feels like a castle!"

David smiles, looking pleased that I approve of his restaurant choice, and takes a seat across from me. "It's one of my favorite restaurants in the city," he says as he unfolds his cloth napkin and places it in his lap.

"How do you have access to this private room? Do you know the owner?"

He clears his throat and shifts in his chair like he's uncomfortable with the question. He mutters something quietly that I can't quite make out.

"What was that?" I ask, leaning in closer to hear better this time.

"I *am* the owner," He shrugs. "Of the building anyway. It's one of my real estate properties. But the building is leased to the restaurant manager."

My eyebrows shoot up. I didn't realize he owned real estate; I thought he just did finance stuff. "Wait, *one* of your real estate properties?"

He fidgets uncomfortably again. "Yes. I own a few other properties... they're all leased and managed by other individuals. This is the only restaurant though."

"Fascinating." I prop my elbows on the table and rest my face in my palms while I study him. "So, what are some of the other properties?"

He grabs the pitcher of water and fills his glass and mine. "Umm... one's an apartment complex and another is a convention center. Nothing terribly interesting." He takes a drink of his water.

He acts slightly uncomfortable telling me about the real estate properties he owns, and there's something really charming about that. I like that he's humble and doesn't invest in real estate to impress people but just because he likes it. Or maybe it's a challenge for him?

"Wow, you're quite the entrepreneur," I quirk an eyebrow and take a sip of my own water.

"Just like you." He smiles. "Anyway, enough about my boring real estate... let's talk about your wildly successful Peru article. It was up to six thousand comments last I checked."

I blow out a deep breath and shake my head. "It's so crazy. I've never had an article blow up like this before." I bite my bottom lip, contemplating whether or not to tell him about the Monaco Hotel sponsorship, but decide to go for it. “I had several emails for new sponsorships too... one from a hotel chain.”

David’s head snaps to attention and he sets his water glass down. “Wow, that’s great. Which hotel chain?”

“Monaco Hotel Inc.,” I roll my lips together to keep my expression neutral. “They’re offering me all-inclusive trips to their hotels as well as compensation for articles I write featuring their hotels, restaurants, and spa services.”

“Monaco... that’s incredible. My parents love staying at their hotels.” He smiles and his eyes soften.

He looks genuinely happy for me, which makes my heart flutter even more than his kisses do. I’ve never had anyone be so supportive of my travel website, and it means more to me than he could ever know.

“I’m pretty excited about the offer. But my parents aren’t going to be happy.” My shoulders slump and I lean back into the plush velvet chair. “Traveling full time would mean I couldn’t work at Abuela’s anymore, and to them, that’s like me choosing myself over my family.”

“That definitely makes your decision complicated,” he says with a sigh.

I nod my head to agree with him.

A waiter knocks, opens the door, and steps inside the room. Wearing the same uniform of suspenders, white shirt and trousers as the bartenders.

“Mr. Windell, what a pleasure.” He smiles congenially. “Would you like your usual bourbon, sir?”

“You know me too well, Mark,” David tells him with a small laugh.

Mark turns toward me, "And what would the lady like to drink?"

I pause for a moment, wanting to see if David is the type to order for me. Because I hate that. He meets my gaze and raises an eyebrow, as if urging me to order what I want.

"Do you have sangria?" I ask the waiter, realizing we don't have menus.

"We do, yes." The waiter, Mark, looks down at our table then over at David. "Would you two like some menus?"

"A menu for the lady would be great. I don't need one."

"Of course. I'll be right back with your drinks and a menu for the lady," Mark says before turning on his heel and leaving us alone again.

I smirk at David. "I take it you come here pretty often? Is this where you bring all of your dates?"

David's shoulders begin to shake and he erupts into laughter. I don't think I've ever seen him laugh this hard. His head even falls back while he laughs. I watch him in amusement, waiting for him to answer my question.

He quiets down and takes another sip of water. "Isa, you're the only date I've ever brought here. And I probably haven't even been on a date in at least a year." He huffs out a laugh.

My eyebrows draw together in confusion. "What? Why?"

"I don't exactly exude the debonair charisma women like." He smirks and gives me a look like he's daring me to disagree.

I giggle at his answer, remembering our interactions before I realized he was actually a decent human. "Okay… but you're so… " I stumble over my words and use my hand and wave it around in his direction. "Handsome, and well spoken, and intelligent—"

He cuts me off before I can go on. "Someone would have to take the time to get to know me to know that… well, except the handsome part." He winks at me and I laugh.

Mark comes back in with our drinks and a menu. We offer our thanks and he exits the room again.

David takes a sip of his bourbon and closes his eyes to savor it. When he opens his eyes again, he pins me with a serious look. "How about you?"

I take a sip of my sangria, which is amazing. David continues speaking, "You go on dates frequently, don't you?"

His assumption surprises me and my sangria goes down the wrong pipe, making me cough and splutter. I take my cloth napkin from my lap and dab at the corners of my mouth. "Uh, I mean… I've been on more dates this last year than you have… but I don't go out with a different guy every night of the week."

"I didn't mean to offend… it's just that you're so outgoing, and… well, stunning. I thought you must get asked out all the time."

My cheeks heat at his compliment. When David gives a compliment, it's because he's being honest, not because he thinks it's expected.

"Thank you." I smile at him then reach for my menu and open it, covering my blush from his sight as I peruse the dinner options.

The door opens once more, and I expect it to be Mark coming to take our order… but it's an attractive couple, probably in their fifties. They look strangely familiar.

"David! We've missed you!" The woman rushes toward him and places a hand on each side of his face.

"Mom? Dad?" He groans and shimmies out of her hands. "What are you guys doing here?"

Chapter Twenty-one

David

I'm staring slack-jawed at my parents, who've just interrupted the only date I've had in over a year. Do parents have a sensor that goes off about these things?

"We tracked you on the *Find My Friends* app! Isn't that neat?" Mom says excitedly.

Dad grins at me, neither of them noticing my date yet, apparently. "Technology these days, it's incredible."

I blink a few times, hoping they'll disappear. "Uh yeah, incredible."

Mom finally notices Isa and gasps. "Oh my goodness, are you on a date? You're his neighbor, right?"

Isa looks at me with a mischievous grin and sticks her hand out in front of my mother to shake her hand. "Yes, Isabella. I finally got the nerve to ask this big hunk over here on a date." She gestures toward me with her thumb.

My mom looks delighted and starts to speak, but I quickly stand from my seat and interrupt. "Isabella, you remember my parents, Ted and Diane? Mom and Dad, this is Isabella. Now that everyone's introduced, why don't you guys go find your own table... preferably in a different restaurant."

I place one hand on my dad's shoulder and the other on my mom's and guide them in the direction of the door.

My mother giggles. "Oh, I'm sorry. We didn't mean to embarrass you!"

"We were just anxious to hear about your trip and couldn't wait until Sunday to see you," Dad explains. "We assumed you were dining alone, as usual," he whispers, like dining alone is horrifying.

Mom turns and walks back toward Isabella; she's short enough to duck right under my arm. Damn it.

"Oh, Isabella! Why don't you come with David to our family dinner on Sunday? We have dinner every Sunday as a family, or we try to!" Mom chuckles and pats Isabella's shoulder. "It's hard to round up all of my children these days."

Isa nods and starts to stand up. "Oh, I wouldn't miss it for the world!"

I withhold a groan. "You can stay seated, Isa. My parents are leaving," I say, staring my parents down with a glare.

"They might like to join us, David," she says in a whisper that's obviously loud enough for my parents to hear.

"Absolutely not."

My mom giggles at Isa's comment. "Oh, David, I like her!"

I point to the exit without saying a word.

"Okay, okay." Mom throws her hands up in defeat like I'm being ridiculous.

She and my father wave at us before walking out the door and closing it behind them. I stand with one palm on the door to make sure they don't come back in and use the other to massage my temples. Isabella bursts into laughter behind me and I turn around to look at her.

"I'm glad one of us is amused," I say, narrowing my eyes at her. This only makes her laugh harder.

"The Find My Friends app?" She laughs. "Trust me, I know what it's like to have overbearing parents... but allowing your parents to stalk you?"

Pulling my phone out of my back pocket, I go straight to the app and press delete. "There. Fixed that."

"So, what should I wear to family dinner?" She bats her eyelashes at me.

"You do not have to come to family dinner; don't let my mother steamroll you into that."

"I really don't mind," She tells me with a genuine smile. "And your family seems fun."

I wrinkle my nose. "They *can* be fun."

"But not as fun as you?" she asks, a twinkle in her eye telling me she's teasing.

"Obviously. No one is as fun as me," I say with a stoney expression, making her laugh.

The door opens again and I stand abruptly, almost knocking my bourbon over. Mark walks in and looks at me with a concerned expression. "Are you guys ready to order, or should I come back?"

I sigh and rest my hands on my hips. "Sorry, Mark. I thought it was my parents again. Could you guys keep them out of here... please?"

"I'm so sorry, Mr. Windell. I'll let everyone know not to let your parents in here. I don't know how they snuck past us."

"It's fine." I take my seat again. "Isa, are you ready to order?"

"Yes, I'll have the six ounce steak, cooked medium." She glances at me over the top of her menu and whispers, "Can we get dessert too?"

The edge of my mouth pulls up into a smile. "Of course, order whatever you'd like."

"And I'll also have the molten lava cake... a la mode," She tells Mark with a big smile.

He smiles back at her. Who wouldn't?

"Make that two molten lava cakes. And I'll have my usual as well. Thank you, Mark."

He nods his head in my direction, takes the menu from Isa and leaves us.

"You know, he would've come back and offered dessert after we ate dinner," I tell her before taking a sip of my drink.

She shrugs one of her bare shoulders, drawing my attention to her bronze skin. Her skin always looks so warm and inviting, along with her big brown eyes. Which are exactly the color of the molten lava cake. Yum... I've always had a weakness for chocolate—and Isabella Romero, apparently.

"Always eat dessert first. Life is short."

"Sometimes I wish I could be as free-spirited as you... or my brother, Brooks." I lean back in my chair and her eyes are locked on mine, like she's staring straight into my soul.

"I actually love how steady and responsible you are," she says, then pauses, rubbing a finger along the edge of her sangria glass. Her nails are painted bright red to match her dress and lips. "I wish I could be more like that. It makes me feel... safe."

My heartbeat quickens at her statement. The fact that she feels safe with me gives me an unexplainable sense of pride. She takes a drink of her sangria, looking up at me through her long lashes. She sets her drink down and breathes out a small laugh.

"Who would've thought the two of us would have nice things to say about each other?"

I laugh, dipping my chin and closing my eyes. "Yeah, I can hardly believe it myself."

After enjoying our meal then chatting by the fireplace for a while, I drive us back to my place and park in the driveway.

I walk around and open her door for her. "Do you want to come in?" I ask her, not wanting to say good-night yet.

This morning I was trying so hard to talk myself out of pursuing this woman, thinking that we're too opposite. That we'd never work long-term. But the more I learn about her, the more I realize how many similarities we have. I feel like she understands me in a way no one else has.

She steps out of the vehicle and looks up at my front door and then back at me. "I want to, but I'm working tomorrow. I'm going in early to help our chef get everything prepared for the weekend."

Her eyes aren't filled with fire like they are when she's talking about traveling or something she's passionate about. Instead, they look droopy and a little sad. I can't help but wonder if she's apprehensive about seeing her parents tomorrow. She begins walking toward her front door and I walk next to her.

"Are your parents going to give you a hard time?" I ask before allowing my hand to brush lightly against hers. Testing the waters to see if she might let me hold her hand… and she makes my entire evening by sliding her hand into mine.

"Probably. But putting it off won't help. And I need to talk to them about this new opportunity to travel full time." She takes a deep breath and releases it in a heavy sigh.

My heart twists inside my chest. My brain is happy for her and the opportunities she's being presented… but my heart wants to keep her here, living a few steps away from me.

"That's going to be a difficult conversation." I give her hand a gentle squeeze. "I'm here if you need to vent after work."

We arrive on her front porch and face each other. She rubs her arms like she's chilled from the evening air. I want so badly to pull her into my arms and wipe the sad look off her face, but I don't want to move too fast. Especially if she's leaving soon. I have no idea what a long-distance relationship even looks like.

"Thank you." She steps toward me and brings her hand up and presses it to my cheek. Her thumb caresses my jaw and I resist the urge to close my eyes and lean into her touch like Mo does when I pet him.

She leans in, clearly wanting me to kiss her, and I can't possibly resist those plump red lips I've stared at all night. I slide both of my hands into her hair and then press my lips to hers.

My hands move from her hair to her neck and then over her bare shoulders. Her skin is so smooth and warm, even silkier than I imagined it was after sitting across from her all evening and stealing glances at her bare skin. I allow my hands to drop slowly from her shoulders then trail down her arms, causing goosebumps to appear along her skin.

I then grab onto her tiny waist, which has been hidden underneath her ruffled dress. Surprisingly, that just made the dress all the sexier. Like a tease.

I've never felt so reckless, never kissed with such wild abandon. My normally controlled and smooth exterior is torn to shreds by Isabella Romero.

I might make her feel safe, but she makes me feel out of control... in a good way.

Chapter Twenty-two

Isabella

Early the next morning, I walk inside Abuela's. After a week off it's nice to be back, it really is. This place is like home to me in some strange way. It's a big part of my family and working together is familiar and comfortable.

If only my heart didn't long for the unfamiliar, for the adventures yet to be had.

As expected, my parents are in my father's office. They're both seated, Papa in his office chair, and Mama in a folding chair pulled up next to him.

When I walk inside, they're already looking up at the door frame, like they've been awaiting my arrival.

"Hey!" I say with a smile, genuinely happy to see them after being away.

My father stands from his seat and walks around his desk to give me a big hug. "Good to have you back, Bella." He says before placing a kiss on top of my head.

My mother offers no such greeting. She keeps a serious expression on her face. "Glad you made it *home*," she says, emphasizing the word *home*. "Although it would've been nice for you to stop in last night and see if we needed any extra help."

I keep a smile firmly on my face, refusing to let her ruin my day. "Sorry, I had things to catch up on and then I had plans in the evening."

She closes her eyes shut and sighs irritably. "The only thing you need to catch up on is helping your family."

"My dear," Papa starts, trying to ease the tension. "Can't we talk about this later?"

"No, we've already waited a week!" Mama stands to her feet, her jaw set in a hard line. "This traveling stops now. Your father and I aren't getting any younger, and you need to be training to manage this place when we retire."

I scoff. "You guys aren't even fifty yet."

"It takes time to learn how to manage a restaurant. Years. From now on, you'll get two weeks off each year. That's it." She lifts her chin as if daring me to defy her.

Stand up for yourself. This is your life and no one can tell you how to live it. I straighten my posture and look Mama directly in the eyes. "And what if I don't agree to your terms?"

"Then I guess we'll know you chose yourself over this family," she states without emotion and then walks out of the room.

Papa groans and runs a hand down his face in frustration. "Why can't you two just get along?"

My nostrils flare with anger and I too leave the office before I say something I'll regret. I walk back to the breakroom to clock in and grab my apron, taking a few deep breaths before heading to the kitchen to help Marco. Chopping vegetables and scrubbing dishes will help me work off some of this pent-up anger.

I storm through the kitchen door, my face heated in anger. Marco spins to see who entered his domain and arches an eyebrow when he sees my angry expression.

"Your mother?"

I nod and he hands me a large knife and points to a giant pile of onions that need diced. Perfect, now I can release hot, angry tears and no one will know it's not caused by the onions.

Marco is a few feet away from me, seasoning steak and chicken. He glances at me sympathetically and gives me a little smile. I smile back, not wanting to take my frustration out on him, then concentrate on the onions.

With every slice I question my place in this family, and wonder why Abuela's has to be part of it. Why can't I choose for myself what I do to make a living like everyone else does? Mama acts like I'm the crowned princess preparing to rule a small country. At the end of the day, this is *just* a restaurant, *just* a job. My love for my family has absolutely nothing to do with this place.

Why can't Mama see that? She's so wrapped up in her love of this restaurant that it's trickled over into every aspect of her life. Like everything is connected to Abuela's, but it's not. Not to me. My parents could sell the restaurant tomorrow to someone who wanted to turn it into a Chuck E. Cheese, and I'd love them just the same.

Not only that, but Rosa has excellent management skills, and she loves working here. She even implemented the iPad system that has streamlined our business. If my parents weren't so focused on tradition, they'd see she's the best fit for taking over this place. If that's what she wants, which I'm pretty sure it is.

Ten onions in and I have a steady stream of tears streaming down my cheeks. Partly because of the onions, partly because of my mother.

I use my free arm to wipe at my face before I continue dicing each onion. It takes me at least an hour to finish them. My face is ruddy and my eyes burn. I dump them into a large container and secure the lid then walk over to the sink, wash my hands and arms well, then splash water on my face. I'm patting my face dry with a dish towel when my sisters burst into the kitchen.

They're both grinning and rush toward me. "Bella!" Lily squeals and wraps her arms around me.

Rosa wraps her arms around us both and I close my eyes, enjoying this moment with my sisters. If I end up traveling full time, I will miss this so much.

We pull away from each other, all of us giddy and smiling.

"How was your trip? I read the article on your website, of course, but I want to hear anything you left out." Lily says, clapping her hands together.

"Have you read my travel articles?" I ask her, my eyes widening in surprise. I never had the impression my sisters were against my website, but I had no idea they kept up with it.

Lily crosses her arms, looking perturbed at my question. "You thought we didn't read your articles?"

Rosa interjects, "We're your sisters. We'll support whatever you're passionate about! Just like you would for us."

My eyes blur with tears and Lily puts her arm around me. "You've done a great job with your website. And you're a really talented writer."

Rosa nods. "The way you write about your travels always makes me want to go visit whatever place you're writing about!"

"Really?" I ask, looking between the two of them. "Mama and Papa are so against it, I guess I wasn't really sure what you two thought of it."

"I subscribe to your website too, Bella." Marco bellows from the other side of the kitchen where he's tossing a salad. "Your sisters are right; you have a gift for writing."

I smile at him and another tear breaks free and runs down my cheek. "Thanks, guys. I actually received a sponsorship opportunity where I could travel and write full time."

"No way! That's amazing," Rosa says, leaning back against the stainless steel countertop. "You should go for it."

I bite my bottom lip. "I really want to."

"Do it! Mama will accept it if she has no other choice," Lily adds, looking way more confident about that than I feel.

Rosa grimaces like she feels the same way I do. I sigh and slump against the counter next to her. "I want to please Mama and Papa, *and* follow my dreams... but it feels like I have to choose one or the other."

My sisters look at me sympathetically, all of us knowing how stubborn our mother is. Courtney walks into the kitchen and grins when she sees me. "Good to have you back!" She ties her apron around her waist without breaking eye contact. "Loved your Peru article!"

I chuckle and my sisters and Marco join in. "See?" Lily tells me with a tilt of her head.

"Thanks, Court! It was an amazing trip." I smile to myself, thinking of the first kiss I shared with David on the mountain top.

Courtney crosses her arms over her chest and arches an eyebrow. "Alright let's hear it. I can tell from that dreamy look on your face you met a guy on this trip."

My sisters study me and I roll my eyes. "You're right," Rosa says, pointing to my face. "She's blushing."

"I am not!"

"Are too," Lily agrees with Rosa.

"I can see the blush from all the way over here," Marco adds.

I roll my lips between my teeth, trying to keep the stupid grin off my face that thoughts of David seem to put there. "Okay, there's a guy. But I didn't meet him on the trip."

The girls lean in, anticipation in their wide eyes. Marco stops his work and waits for me to continue.

"You remember my grumpy neighbor?"

Rosa wrinkles her nose. "The accountant?"

I nod. "So the first day of the hike, I look behind me… and there he is."

Lily gasps. "On the same trip??"

"Yep! And we ended up sharing a tent."

Courtney rubs her hands together. "Oh, this is getting good."

"And on the last night… I kissed him."

They all gasp, even Marco. "What did he do?" Rosa asks.

"He pulled me into his lap and kissed me back."

The ladies all sigh in unison and Marco whistles loudly.

"You definitely left all the juicy details out of your Peru article," Courtney says with a giggle.

Mama bursts into the kitchen, Papa trailing closely behind her. All of us stand up straight and disperse amongst the kitchen, making ourselves look busy.

"I'm gonna go set the tables," Courtney announces befores grabbing the bucket of napkins and silverware, then exits the kitchen. She shoots me a secret smile right before the swinging doors close behind her.

Mama looks between me and my sisters with a stern expression. "There's much work to be done, girls."

"Yes, Mama," Lily says sweetly.

My mother gives us one more speculative glance before walking out of the kitchen toward the main restaurant area. Papa smiles at us then follows her.

I can hardly remember a time when Mama looked happy, like she was actually enjoying life instead of working all the time. She's always so serious, I wonder what she'd be like if she let my sisters, or even Papa, take on more responsibility around here.

Chapter Twenty-three

Isabella

Sunday morning my sisters and I wake up and get ready for Mass together. They spent the night at my place so we could catch up. On Sundays we always go to Mass together as a family, *another* tradition. I haven't made it to Mass in two weeks, which is just one more strike against me.

Once we're all dressed and ready in our Sunday best, we walk outside to my car. Trying to be discreet, I sneak a glance at David's house and see him walking down the solid wooden steps of his front porch. His movements are precise, calculated even. He bends at the waist to retrieve his Sunday morning paper, his slim fingers reaching for the paper with the elegance of a historian handling a rare artifact. He's not wearing a robe or pajamas, but is ready for the day in a grey and navy plaid button up and tan slacks. He spots me watching him and grins, using the paper in his hand to wave at me. My sisters giggle behind me.

"Good morning, David!" Lily says in a high-pitched voice, like she's trying to sound like me.

Rosa wiggles her fingers at him in a silly wave, adding a wink for extra drama.

David quirks a brow, looking a little confused at their antics. "Um, good morning."

"Are we still on for the barbecue tonight?" I ask, ignoring my sister's tittering in the background.

"It's not too late to back out if you want to." He brings his palm to his forehead and chokes out a cough. "Actually, I think I might be coming down with something."

"Not a chance. I'm dying to get to know the woman who stalks her adult children through an app."

He groans. "Alright. At least I can relish the fact that I can bring a date and Brooks can't."

I rub my hands together and do my best evil laugh. "Ooh this will be fun. Should I hang all over you and shower you with compliments?"

"I'd expect nothing less," he says in his dry tone that I'm starting to love more and more.

I turn and see my sisters are now in the car waiting for me. "We better head out. Mama will have our heads if we're late to Mass."

"See you tonight." His eyes soften, no longer cold and dry with his strange humor. "You look beautiful."

I smile at him and wave as I duck inside my car, wishing I was spending the day with David.

My sisters and I walk into St. Andrew's Church and find our parents easily since they've sat in the same spot in the second row for as long as I can remember. We shuffle our way into the pew next to them and my mother smiles at me. The smile I remember from when I was a little girl and she wasn't constantly pressuring me to take over Abuela's. Back when we were just mother and daughter, not owner and hopeful-future-owner.

Her hair is down today. She wears it shorter than she did when she was younger. It now comes to her clavicle instead of streaming halfway down her back. Mama is a beautiful woman, but I can see how stress has aged her. Her tanned skin that used to glow like the sun now looks pale from lack of being outside. She has small grooves in the skin around her eyes and instead of smile lines, she has frown lines.

My heart tightens as I smile back at her and take my seat. Realizing that Mama probably wants me to take over the restaurant so she can finally have a break.

But still, why does it have to be me just because I'm the oldest? Rosa was meant to be a manager, not me. I know Lily is too young to run Abuela's, being that she's only twenty. But Rosa is just a few years younger than myself.

Papa is elated on the other side of Mama, he leans over her and gives me a pat on the knee. "Good to see all my girls together." He winks.

Rosa clears her throat from my opposite side and I turn to look at her. She jerks her head to the side like she's motioning for me to look at something. I'm too distracted by how ridiculous she looks to notice what she's trying to convey.

Finally, Lily leans over and whispers, "It's Fabio."

My eyes shoot up to see the man who came to the restaurant over a week ago. He smiles at me, obviously not surprised to see me here. Then he shuffles into our row, past my two sisters and squeezes between myself and Rosa.

I gape at him, not knowing what to say and wondering how someone could be so presumptuous that I'd want to sit by him.

Mama leans over and smiles at him. "Fabio, so glad you could join us today!"

"My pleasure! Thank you for inviting me," he tells her, then turns to me. "Wonderful to see you again, Isabella."

I give him a forced smile in response, not trusting myself to say anything nice to him. Taking a deep breath through my nose, then blowing it out through my mouth, I turn my head slowly toward my mother.

I'm looking at her through narrowed eyes, my nostrils flaring with barely contained rage. She calmly keeps her eyes in front of her at the pulpit, where Father Joseph is getting ready for the homily.

"Be nice. The only reason you're not content staying in one place is because you haven't fallen in love yet. I'm simply helping the process along," Mama whispers to me without making eye contact.

"I'm already seeing someone," I whisper back through gritted teeth.

Mama's head snaps over to look at me. "What? Who? When?"

"Do we really have to do this now?" I angle my head backward, gesturing to the man next to me.

She purses her lips, making her frown lines even more prominent. "We'll discuss this as soon as possible. Is he even Catholic?"

I roll my eyes and release a heavy sigh, just as everyone in the church has quieted down in anticipation of Father Joseph to walk out from the side door by the pulpit. Father Joseph glances at me, quirking one eyebrow in an annoyed stare.

I do the sign of the cross and he clears his throat before announcing which passage he'll be reading from today.

Fabio leans toward me and whispers in my ear, "You look nice today."

Not only does his breath smell like a weird mixture of garlic and coffee, but he's one of those guys who thinks *nice* is a compliment. How about sexy, gorgeous, breathtaking, your body is almost as beautiful as your brain... take your pick! Any adjective besides *nice*.

Okay, honestly, I don't want any compliments from Fabio whatsoever, especially if I have to be subjected to the stench of his breath.

The wooden pew we're seated on seems harder and more uncomfortable than ever, with Fabio sitting on my left side and Mama on my right. My spine is tense and my butt is already getting sore. I look up above Father Joseph to study the beautiful stained glass to distract myself. The ornate window depicts a scene of Mary and Jesus walking together. The glass is a rainbow of colors and I've loved it since I was a child. The chapel has smaller stained glass windows lining the walls of the chapel, all of them colorful and show a different saint.

I listen intently to Father Joseph's holy reading, even closing my eyes in reverence. Mostly so Fabio will leave me alone. Once Mass is over, which seemed to run abnormally long today, I scurry out of the pew as quickly as possible.

Mama glares at me. I wrinkle my nose and smile apologetically. "Please excuse me, I have to use the ladies' room."

My parents stare at me with unconvinced expressions. "Sorry! Too much coffee this morning," I say, huffing out an awkward laugh before rushing to the bathroom, which is conveniently located by the front doors. Close to freedom.

I almost take out an elderly woman when I open the bathroom door and seek out an empty stall to hide in. After apologizing profusely, I lock myself in an empty stall and take a deep breath. A light tapping sound comes from the stall next to me.

"Bella?" Lily whispers. "Want some help escaping?"

Thank goodness for sisters. "Yes, please."

"I'll tell Mama I checked on you and you're not feeling well. You can head home in your car and we'll leave with Mama and Papa."

"I owe you big time," I whisper back.

She giggles. "I'll make sure you pay up one of these days."

Chapter Twenty-four

David

"Wait, so you hid in the bathroom?" I ask Isa on the drive over to my parent's house for our Sunday family barbeque.

"Yes!" She covers her face with her hands. "It was awful."

I chuckle, picturing her escaping to the restroom to get away from some guy named Fabio.

"It's not funny!" She slaps my shoulder with her tiny hand. A text from my mom pops up on the screen in my Land Rover.

Isa reads the message out loud since I'm driving. "'Are you on your way, I can't see your location on the app.'" Then she bursts out laughing. "Wow. At least *both* of our moms are insane and we can commiserate."

"You have no idea," I say dryly. "My mom has a wedding Pinterest board for each of us."

I glance over at her and her eyes are wide. "Oh no, I bet mine does too."

We laugh as I pull into my parent's driveway.

Isa gasps, taking in their large historical home. "David! You didn't tell me your parents lived like *this*." She mutters something under her breath that sounds like, "You guys really are the Cullens from *Twilight*."

"I still have no idea who that is." I turn off the ignition and turn toward her. "But I assure you, my family is just a normal, somewhat crazy, Midwestern family."

She shoots me a sassy expression. "With above average intelligence, talent, and looks?"

"Precisely."

Isa rolls her eyes and exits the vehicle. Snickering to myself, I open my car door and follow after her. I place my hand on her elbow and gently guide her toward the gate to the backyard.

I'm not used to being nervous when I come to my parent's house, but my anxiety is creeping in, making its appearance as a sweat-mustache on my freshly shaven face.

Isa stops abruptly and grabs my hand, pulling me to a stop as well. "Hey, you okay?" Her eyes shift as she studies my face and the set of my shoulders.

I rub the nape of my neck with my free hand. "Yeah. I've just never brought anyone to meet my family."

"Listen, we don't have to do this. I didn't mean to push my way into your family barbeque. I just thought your family seemed fun and wanted to see them again." She rubs her hand up and down my arm in a soothing motion.

I've never been a touchy-feely person. If anything, it makes me even more uncomfortable or stressed. But with Isa, it's different. Her touch is soft and calming. I find myself craving more and more, like I can never get enough.

"No, it's okay. I'm realizing that just because something is out of my comfort zone, that doesn't mean it's bad." I gently grab the hand she's using to rub my arm and bring her hand to my lips and kiss the top of it. "I'm glad you want to get to know my family. And I have no doubt they'll love you."

She bites her bottom lip. "Are you sure?"

"I'm sure," I answer quickly, and I am. But there's a slight hesitation since she's probably leaving soon. What if the only woman I bring to meet my family leaves me to travel the world? I place my hand on her lower back and urge her toward the wrought iron gate.

After typing in the code, I open the gate for her, and when she walks into the yard she gasps again like she did when we pulled into the driveway.

"Are you serious right now?" she whispers with wide eyes. "This is what I picture the gardens of Versailles to look like!"

I scoff. "That's a major exaggeration."

"David? Is that you?" my mom yells from around the corner.

"Yes, It's me," I call back, rounding the corner with Isa right next to me.

My parents are both grinning widely at the sight of me... with a woman. The rest of the family is silent. Madden's and Brooks' mouths are agape, Drew and

Sophie have knowing smirks on their faces, and Odette is too busy with the boys to notice what's going on.

When she finally gets Bradford situated in his seat, she looks up and her expression matches her husband's.

"Is this a joke?" Brooks finally breaks the silence. He crossed his arms and narrows his eyes at me. "You already won the bet. You're not required to keep shocking us."

Isa loops her arm through mine. "Where's *your* date this evening, Brooks?" she asks him in an angelically sweet voice. I bite the insides of my cheeks to keep from laughing.

"Very funny." Brooks smirks. "I can see why you didn't like her at first, David." He winks at her so she knows he's joking.

"Brooks!" Mom lectures him, "Don't scare her off! This is the first girl David has brought home!"

I close my eyes, hoping to disappear entirely. Nothing like your own mother doubting your romantic capabilities.

Sophie and Odette walk over and hug Isabella, giving her a warm welcome.

"So good to see you again! How was Peru?" Sophie asks.

Odette looks confused and her eyes shift from me to Isa. "Wait, Isabella was in Peru too?"

Drew walks up behind Sophie and waggles his eyebrows at me.

Madden stalks over and stands next to Odette. "Sounds like you two have some explaining to do."

With the adults distracted, all of the kids have now abandoned the table and are running around the yard like they just took shots of energy drinks.

Dad, who's standing on the large patio next to the grill, waves his arm in the air. "Let's sit down first. The food is ready." He cups his hands around his mouth and yells, "Kids! Come back to the table!"

The four of them look up and reluctantly walk back to the patio.

My mother points to the two seats at the center of the long outdoor table on the patio. "David and Isabella, you two sit here. We want to hear all the details!"

I sigh and glance over at Isa. She's looking up at me with her round, chocolate-brown eyes and all my annoyance melts away. My shoulders relax and I walk with Isa to take our designated seats at the table.

My parents make everyone's plates and distribute the food as Isa tells my family all about how we both ended up on the same trip and sharing a tent. She gives all the details, animatedly talking with her hands. Of course, their favorite part is the llama sneaking into our tent and licking my face. The whole table erupts in laughter, even the kids giggle at her story.

"Wow, David in a tent with not one, but two females," Brooks says, shaking his head in disbelief.

"Well, I have to make up for you not being able to date," I deadpan.

His mouth forms a straight line. "Ha. Funny."

My parents then inform everyone they stumbled upon us on our first date and how embarrassed I was. Which, according to my mother, was adorable.

"You have to turn your location off when you're on a date," Madden says with a chuckle. "Rookie mistake."

Brooks, who's next to him, bumps Madden's shoulder with his own. "We have a few tricks to teach you about dating without Mom and Dad bursting in."

"Don't ruin this for us," Mom whisper-yells to Brooks from across the table.

I feel Isa slide her hand into mine under the table, lacing our fingers together. We give each other a secret smile. She acclimated to new people and places so effortlessly. I can picture her coming to our family barbecue every Sunday or hanging out with Odette and Sophie.

Odette interrupts our private moment. "So, Isabella, what do you do?"

She smiles at Odette but continues holding my hand under the table. I rub the back of her soft hand with my thumb, the back and forth motion making me feel at ease and relaxed, despite the onslaught of questions from my family.

"Well, I work at my family's restaurant right now." She pauses as if she's considering whether to continue. "But I'm actually hoping to take my travel website full time soon."

My shoulders tense and my thumb pauses on the back of her hand. I swallow the lump in my throat that seems to lodge itself there everytime I think of Isa traveling full time. Of course, I want her to do what she loves. And she's been offered an amazing opportunity... but this thing between us is so unexpected, and so good. I don't want to think about her leaving.

"That's so cool, what an adventure!" Odette tells her, then continues asking questions about her website.

Sophie and Drew look at each other and then at me, both with the same look of sympathy on their faces. It's like even they know a long distance relationship won't work and I'll be left here, gutted.

By the time we're finished eating, the sun is setting, displaying a brilliant reflection of oranges and pinks throughout the sky. The string lights are gleaming and the cicadas are chirping. The kids have quieted down and my little niece Samantha is asleep in Drew's arms. Frank Sinatra's *Fly Me to the Moon* plays through the outdoor speakers and I find myself wishing every evening looked like this. Except in my imagination everyone is gathered at me and Isa's house, and after they leave, we'll sway to the music together under the starry night sky.

What has gotten into me? Starry night sky? I've never been a romantic, and I can't start now. Not when the woman I want to romance is likely to leave the country soon.

Clearing my throat, I interrupt the ambiance of the evening. "Well, I should get Isa home." I stand from my seat. "And I have an early meeting in the morning."

Isa scoots her chair back and stands next to me. "So I shouldn't put any flamingos in your yard tonight?" Isa asks, just loud enough that only I can hear her.

"I would appreciate that," I tell her with a smirk.

We say our goodbyes to my family and drive back to our neighborhood. The drive is quiet, not necessarily uncomfortable, but both of us are obviously lost in our own thoughts.

Parking in my driveway, I exit my Land Cruiser before walking over to the passenger side and opening Isa's door for her. She holds my hand again as I walk her to her front porch.

"Your family is great, David," she says, pausing by her front door. As usual, Mo is scratching from the other side of the door.

"Thanks for coming with me. It was really nice having you there," I tell her honestly. "They loved you, like I knew they would."

Her eyebrows draw together slightly. "Then why do you look sad?"

I sigh and nervously push my glasses up higher on the bridge of my nose. "This is going to sound ridiculous." I shuffle from one foot to the other. "I know we've only been on one date... but I have this really great feeling about us. Feelings aren't usually my barometer, I prefer facts. But there's something special here."

She takes a deep breath. "I have the same feeling."

"You should accept that sponsorship from Monaco Hotels, live your dreams, travel the world, and write incredible articles about all of it to inspire people. I want that for you, I really do... I'm just not sure where I would fit into all of that."

The corners of her round eyes appear to slant down, making her look like a sad little kitten. I want to scoop her up, take her home with me, and tell her everything will be okay. But she's not a kitten, she's a grown woman with an adventurous spirit that would feel suffocated if

I tried to keep her here. And the last thing I want is to make her feel that way when her parents are already accomplishing that.

"I want to be with you, make my parents proud, *and* have a job that I love." She closes her eyes and shakes her head slowly. "But I don't know how to make all of those things happen. I feel so overwhelmed."

Facing her, I take both of her hands in mine. "I don't want to make you feel pressured. We can try the long distance thing. Maybe it won't be so bad?"

We both know that's a lie. I can see the doubt in her eyes because it mirrors my own.

"We don't have to figure this out right now. Get some rest and I'll see you tomorrow?" I lean in to kiss her forehead and she wraps her arms around my waist, pressing her cheek against my chest.

Walking back to my house, my heart feels heavy. I hate the thought of Isa being far away from me... but I cannot become another hurdle just getting in the way of her dreams. If I love her, I'll encourage her to pursue her dreams.

Love? I stop abruptly in front of my house. Am I already in love with Isa?

I care for her... deeply. But love? Surely it's too soon for that.

Chapter Twenty-five

Isabella

The next morning I receive a phone call from an international number. I assume it's spam, but answer it anyway.

"Hi, am I speaking with Isabella Romero?" It's a woman's voice with a delightful European accent, possibly French?

"This is her." My coffee has finally finished brewing. I take the pot and start pouring coffee into my new mug that I purchased from the travel company that hosted our Machu Picchu excursion. It has the same design that our guides had on the back of their t-shirts: a llama wearing sunglasses with the words, *Only you can prevent drama*.

"Wonderful! This is Bridget Lecour from Monaco Hotels. Is this a good time to chat?"

I stop mid-pour and thrust the coffee pot back into the coffee maker. "Oh! Yes, now is fine."

"I wanted to follow up with you and see if you received my email?" There's noise in the background like she's at the airport.

"Yes, I did. Sorry I haven't responded. I needed some time to think, but I'm very interested in your offer." I take my coffee mug into the living room and sit on the sofa.

"Fabulous! I actually just arrived in Kansas City for a marketing conference at our hotel here."

I set my mug down on the coffee table and open my laptop so I can make notes if I need to. "Really? That's only a few hours from me."

"I know this is very short notice, but would you be able to come up sometime today or tomorrow? I could show you the hotel and we could discuss the sponsorship contract."

I glance at the clock on my laptop. It's just after nine now, and I don't have to be at work until 4:30. "I could be there by noon today. I just have to be back here for work tonight, so I'll only have a few hours."

"Perfect! I can squeeze you in from twelve to two!" A loud overhead announcement comes over the speaker in the background and she pauses until it's done. "I'll text you the address. Is this a good number?"

"Yes, this is my cell," I tell her, wondering how she got this number in the first place. I suppose it's easy enough to find on Google.

"See you then, Ms. Romero!" The way she says my name with her fancy accent makes it sound so fancy.

We hang up and she texts me the address of the Monaco Hotel in Kansas City.

Three hours later, I'm walking inside Monaco Hotel's luxury restaurant. I had about ten minutes to get ready, so thankfully my hair was still curled from yesterday. I threw on some mascara, deodorant, and an informal black dress and wedge heels. Not too shabby for ten minutes.

The restaurant is spacious, with high ceilings and crystal chandeliers. The front is all glass, facing out toward the busy city street, and filling the space with natural light. Classical music plays softly in the background as people enjoy their lunch. The patrons are all dressed nicely, looking like they just came from work. I glance around at the tables and booths, trying to guess where Bridget might be waiting for me.

"Isabella!" A tall, slender woman with a perfect blonde bob calls from a few yards away. She comes towards me, walking like a model would. She's incredibly stylish and smells amazing when she leans in to do the French cheek-kissing thing.

I make kissy noises like she does, not really knowing what I'm supposed to do. "Aren't you just darling!" she purrs in her accented voice. "Let's have a seat." She gestures toward the table behind her.

"Thank you," I tell her as I slide into my upholstered chair. "The restaurant is beautiful."

"Oh, darling, wait until you see the suites," She smirks before taking a sip of her water. "Order whatever you'd like; lunch is on Monsieur Monaco."

I laugh and take a sip of my own water. "I do love food."

"Perfect," she says, folding her cloth napkin and laying it in her lap. "So, we'd love for you to feature our rooms as well as our restaurants, cocktails, and spa services. The whole shebang!"

"That sounds right up my alley. How many locations does the Monaco Hotel have?" I ask, dreaming of the places I could travel to.

"Great question! We currently have ninety-nine hotels worldwide, but number one hundred is almost finished." She winks. "We're actually planning a big celebration for its opening next week, and would love you to come and write an article about the new location."

"Wow, a hundred. Where is the new one?"

"Venice, Italy." she says it casually, like it's no big deal.

I nod my head, trying to play it cool. "I've heard Venice is lovely."

"You'd love it! It's gorgeous."

The waiter comes and takes our orders, both of us selecting the strawberry chicken salad. I'm a sucker for anything that has blue cheese sprinkled on top.

While we eat, Bridget gives me a rundown of what my contract would entail. Basically, I'd be traveling one week, writing the next, and then repeat in a different location. My stays in any of their hotels will be covered, as well as meals I eat in their restaurants. I can even keep my current sponsorships and add new ones, as long as they're not with competing hotels or spas.

I listen intently while she talks, which isn't difficult since her accent is mesmerizing.

"Anyway, enough about the boring details. Let's go see the rooms, shall we?" She folds her napkin neatly on the table and stands.

I follow her lead and stand next to her. She towers over me; she's probably as tall as David. We walk toward the elevator, which has ornate golden doors, and she pushes the button for the very top floor. Even the inside of the elevator is luxurious, with mirrored walls and mosaic tile floors. When we reach the top floor, we walk out to a wide hallway with only four doors. That probably means these four rooms are gigantic.

Bridget pulls a keycard from a tiny pocket in the waistband of her fitted pencil skirt and opens the nearest door. When we walk into the suite, I have to work hard to keep my expression neutral, and not give away the fact that never in my life have I seen a hotel room like this. At least not in person.

The room consists of floor to ceiling windows, with a magnificent view of the city. Almost everything is white with blush and gold accents. The sofas are white linen and matching arm chairs sit across from them. There are fresh pink peonies in short vases around the room.

"This is gorgeous," I say, attempting to keep the awe out of my voice.

I don't think Bridget buys it because she's watching me with a big grin. "Wait until you see the bedroom."

She walks over to the large white French doors and pulls them open to reveal a giant bed that looks as fluffy as a cloud. I want to run and jump on it and roll around in the pillows. But instead I nod my head and smile professionally and walk inside the bedroom to investigate further.

A beautiful white-washed fireplace graces the area right in front of the bed, with another small sofa next to it. I turn the opposite direction to see a large bathroom with a gorgeous claw-foot tub is right off the large bedroom, with marble floors and more gold accents.

"Wow," My cool facade finally falters. "When can I move in?"

Bridget giggles. "Isn't it gorgeous?" She takes a few long strides and opens another door, this one leading to a walk-in closet. "Obviously, you won't always stay in a suite; they book up pretty fast, but we'd love for you to do write ups about every type of room we offer so travelers of all budgets can see their options."

"That sounds amazing. So what does a regular room look like?"

"Let's go see!" She walks quickly out of the bedroom and toward the door.

I almost have to run to keep up with her.

"Damn it. I'm late." I glance down at my watch for the gazillionth time as I pull into the employee parking behind Abuela's. Hitting Kansas City traffic on my way home caused me to be thirty minutes late for my shift. I didn't even have time to run home and change, so I'm still wearing my dress and wedge heels.

I barely have my car in park before I rush out of the vehicle and toward the back entrance to Abuela's, screeching to a halt when I see my mother there waiting for me.

Her arms are crossed and I swear her frown lines are even deeper than they were yesterday morning at Mass.

"Late again?" Her voice is cold. "This has got to stop."

I square my shoulders and look at her. "Not now, Mama."

"First, you're rude to Fabio. And now you're late... again!" Her nostrils flare with anger.

"Seriously? You promised to stop trying to set me up, then get mad about me being upset?" I yell back.

She steps closer, so she's right in my face. "For your own good! Fabio has a degree in restaurant management; you'll need his help running this place."

"Actually, that won't be necessary."

Her eyes widen. "And why's that?"

"Because I just signed a contract with Monaco Hotels and will begin writing and traveling full time... starting next week."

"So that's it? You're choosing your own selfish dreams over our family?"

"That's the difference between you and I, Mama." I take a deep breath, my chin quivering with emotion. "I don't love you because of the work you do at this restaurant." I point to the building behind us. "I love you because you're my mother. My love for this family has nothing to do with that pile of bricks."

Her chest is heaving as she stares at me. "I've dedicated my life, my evenings, my weekends, everything. To make this place a success and make sure you girls had a good life. So yes, Abuela's *is* a part of my love for you."

"*Part*, Mama. Not *all*."

She seems frozen, unable to speak. We stand there staring at each other for a few seconds before she finally breaks the silence, "If you've already signed a contract, there's no reason for you to work tonight."

She turns away from me and swings the heavy back door open. She steps inside and allows the door to close behind her without looking back at me.

When the door closes and I hear the latch close, it's like I can feel it. Like a slap in the face.

I turn and walk back to my car.

Chapter Twenty-six

David

Monday evening, I'm relaxing on my comfortable couch nursing a bourbon on the rocks, when a belligerent knock comes from my front door.

"What the hell?" I mutter to Mo, who's sitting next to me purring. I don't even bother fighting him when he ends up inside my house anymore.

Reluctantly, I get up and walk over to the front door and fling it open. Ready to give the intruder of my evening a piece of my mind. But when I see Isabella with tears streaming down her face, my grumpy demeanor wilts instantly.

"Isa, what's wrong?" I pull her inside and then into my arms.

She's crying too much to answer, so I walk us over to the sofa and pull her onto my lap. Cradling her into my chest much like I would my little nieces and nephews.

A war of emotions is battling inside of me. There's a softness wanting to comfort her and a hardness wanting to demand, "WHO DID THIS TO YOU?"

I suppress them both and just hold her, rubbing her back gently as her breathing regulates and her tears slow down. I wait until she's ready to talk, just enjoying the feel of her in my arms, in my home, in my heart.

"I met with the marketing director of Monaco Hotels today," she says, finally looking up at me. Her face is red and her eyes are puffy from tears.

I smile down at her. "Really? How'd it go?"

She sighs wistfully. "Amazing. I signed a contract with them."

My heart stills inside of my chest. Not because I'm not happy for her, but because I'm unhappy for myself. Yes, I'm a selfish bastard. Sue me. I want to keep Isabella here in my arms forever.

"Congratulations," I tell her, truly meaning the words despite how much I'll miss her.

"Thank you." She looks over and notices Mo for the first time and shakes her head at him like a parent would a disobedient child.

Mo hops down from the sofa and walks toward us, rubbing against our legs and purring. "He likes me."

She laughs through her tears and then nuzzles back against my chest. "Anyway, I told my mother about the contract and she basically disowned me."

My eyebrows furrow, instantly disliking this woman I've never met. Mothers are tricky creatures, my own included. But what mother would make her own daughter feel so awful for following her heart and doing something she truly loves?

"I'm sorry, Isa. This new opportunity should be celebrated, and your mom ruined it for you."

"Thank you. But it's alright." She pauses and reaches down to give Mo a pat on his furry head. "I think she's just exhausted and wanting to retire. She must've hoped I'd take over soon and she could finally have a break."

"What about your sisters?"

She sighs. "That's the thing. Mama has always expected me to take over because I'm the oldest. But Rosa is the one who really wants it."

"I have a feeling now that you'll be traveling, Rosa will get her chance to shine and show your mom how great she'd be managing Abuela's."

She looks up at me again, her expression looking surprised. "You know what? I bet you're right. I've just always been there, getting in the way."

I chuckle and tighten my arms around her. "That's not necessarily what I meant. But the way your mother is acting isn't healthy, and a parent's love for their child should never be bound to their occupation." Resting my chin on the top of her head, I inhale the scent of her shampoo. The scent I remember all too well from our nights sharing a tent. The tightness in my chest returns, remembering the contract she signed. "So, when do you start traveling?"

"I leave for Venice in five days." She pauses. "I'm staying at Monaco's newest build and writing an article about their Venice location, and their one hundredth location celebration."

I swallow, twice, trying to wet my mouth and throat that has suddenly become as dry as sandpaper. "Wow, that's soon."

She pulls away from me and settles on the couch right next to me so we can talk face to face. "I know it won't be easy, but I don't want things to end between us just because I'll be traveling."

Holding her gaze, I start to reply but stop, not knowing what to say. "Isa… how many weeks a month will you be traveling?"

She blinks a few times, as if registering what I'm really asking. "I mean, probably most of the time… but you can visit me."

I sigh, knowing where this is going but not wanting to make her even more upset. "Visit you where, exactly?"

"Well, most of Monaco's locations are overseas… so I'll probably get a small flat somewhere in Europe."

I nod. "Right. But how often will you be in Kansas?"

Her eyes fill with tears. "Not very often."

One lonesome tear breaks free and streams down her face. I softly brush it away with my thumb. "Listen, we don't have to talk about this tonight. I know it's been a long day for you."

"No." She pulls away from me, her eyes filled with hurt. "Say it."

I pause for a beat, and she tilts her chin in a defiant gesture. "Isa, I'm not going to hold you back from your dreams. You have a talent for writing and a heart for traveling. Not only have you worked hard for this, but you deserve it." I stand and try to close the distance between us, but she backs away from me. "I'm not going to beg you to stay. That would make me just like your mother."

She closes her eyes, more tears escaping through her dark lashes. "David, please don't."

"Don't you get it?" I beg her to see my perspective. "I want you to finally be free. To do what you were meant to do. Of course I want to be together, but my life is here... and a long distance relationship would just distract you from this new life."

"I know it will be hard." Her eyes are pleading and her voice is strained. "But can't we at least try?"

Maybe it's the pessimist in me, but I can't picture how this would ever work between us. Not because I don't want it to, but because our lives are literally going in opposite directions. She's emotional, and she's had a difficult day. I don't want to be the person to make it even worse.

"Listen, what if we take a break? You can get settled in your new job and find a flat. Then we can discuss this again?"

She looks slightly less perturbed, but not much. "A break?" She crosses her arms. "Is this like a Ross and Rachel break?"

I narrow my eyes. "Really? I haven't dated a woman in *years* and that's what you're worried about?"

"What if the next woman who moves in next door catches your fancy?"

"Catches my fancy?" I close my eyes in frustration and massage my temples with my thumb and forefinger. "If another infuriating woman moves in next door, I'll stay far away from her, trust me."

Isa harrumps and keeps her arms crossed. Why does she have to look so adorable when she's irritated? All I can think about is kissing that ridiculous scowl off her face.

Yes, a break will be good for us. "We need some time to breathe and really think about this. Three weeks. That will give us time apart to make a rational decision." I nod my head, like I'm agreeing with myself. Someone has to agree with me, and it's obviously not going to be the woman standing in front of me. "You know, statistically—"

She cuts me off with a groan. "Not with the statistics! Some things can't be decided with numbers, David." She sighs, her expression finally softening. "Three weeks... fine."

Day one of the break: Everything sucks without Isa.

Day two of the break: Mo won't come over anymore unless I coax him with treats.

Day three of the break: I had to watch Isa and her sisters carry all the furniture and packed belongings from Isa's house today. A month ago, I would have rejoiced that I no longer had to deal with her. But now my chest aches with every box they load into the moving truck.

Day four of the break: Isa leaves for Venice tomorrow. We haven't spoken in four days now—

"What are you doing?"

My head jerks up in surprise to see Drew and Brooks standing in my kitchen. "How did you guys get into my house?"

Brooks takes a step toward the table where I'm sitting and chuckles. "Is that a diary?"

Drew slugs him in the shoulder and he winces. "Leave him alone. He's heartbroken." He crosses his arms, pinning Brooks with a serious stare. "Also, there's nothing wrong with a man journaling his feelings. Mental health is important."

I slam my journal shut. Not sure what I was thinking, documenting what's going to be the worst three weeks of my life. It seemed like writing might connect me and Isabella in some cosmic way. Wow, it sounds stupid just thinking it. Next, I'm going to start reading my daily horoscope. What star sign am I even?

"Mom told us to check on you because you haven't left your house in four days," Brooks explains.

I roll my eyes. "Stupid Find My Friends app... They should rename it the 'stalk your kids' app."

Drew shoves his hands into his jean pockets. "She's just worried about you."

Releasing a heavy sigh, I glance at the clock on the stove and see it's already seven and I've forgotten to eat dinner... again.

"Bourbon?" I ask them, standing from the table and walking over to the bar cart.

They nod and I pour us each a glass.

"So what's going on? Last we saw you, you were all heart-eyes over your neighbor," Brooks says, taking a glass of bourbon from the bar cart before I can hand it to him.

"Technically, she's not my neighbor anymore." I chug my bourbon in one big gulp. "She'll be traveling and writing full time now; she got an amazing offer from Monaco Hotels."

"That sucks, I'm sorry, man," Drew says, giving me a hard pat on the back as he takes his glass of bourbon from the bar cart. I turn to pour myself another glass but Drew grabs the bottle. "Why don't we slow it down a bit?"

I shrug and walk into the living room then slump down into an armchair. Brooks and Drew follow me and take a seat on the couch.

"Where's Madden?"

"D.C., remember? He'll be back in a few weeks," Brooks reminds me.

"Oh, right." I think for a beat. "How have those two made the long distance thing work?"

Drew quirks a brow. "They don't really have a choice. Madden goes back and forth between Kansas and D.C. all the time."

"Odette and the boys visit him in D.C. pretty often too," Brooks adds. "I know it's hard on them though, which is why he's not running for another term."

"Yeah, that must be really difficult." I lean forward and rest my forearms on my knees. "Isa and I are taking a break for a few weeks to clear our heads and think about how this can really work."

They nod in unison, neither speaking, probably wanting me to continue. "We were on that trip together and then we lived next door to each other... everything was getting blurry, you know?"

Drew smirks like he knows exactly what I'm talking about. Brooks' eyebrows draw together in a confused expression.

"Anyway, she didn't want to end things and I didn't want to hold her back from this new opportunity... so we settled on taking a break and reevaluating in three weeks."

Drew's face turns to the same look of confusion as Brooks'.

"Do you know what the definition of *insanity* is?" Brooks asks before huffing out a laugh. "Doing the same thing repeatedly and expecting a different outcome."

Drew and Brooks chuckle at my dumbfounded expression. Drew shoves Brooks playfully. "Dude, I always forget you're smart."

"I'm more than just a pretty face!" Brooks lifts his nose in the air haughtily, then turns to me and continues, "You and Isabella are expecting something to change over the next few weeks when neither of you is willing to change the situation."

Drew nods with a sigh. "Insanity."

I stand from my seat so fast the chair scoots a few inches and squeaks on the wood floor. I throw my hands in the air and begin pacing in front of the sofa. I do this so often now, I'm going to wear out a path on the wood floor.

"How am I supposed to change the situation? Lock her in my attic?"

"Or you could go with her." Drew shrugs like what he's suggesting is no big deal.

I scoff. "And what about my house? And my business? And my clients?"

"Okay, we get it. You're a very important person," Brooks says sarcastically. "But seriously, you don't need the money. Your real estate investments and stocks have you set for life."

"B-b-but," I trip over my own words. "I hate new places. As well as most people. I mean, me? Traveling all the time?"

They both look at me silently with smug looks on their faces, like they think this is somehow all sorted out now.

But my family is here. And I like my work... I like my home.

But do I love those things as much as I love Isa?

Yes, *love*. I've been kidding myself, pretending I'm not already in love with the woman. I'm pretty sure I started falling the minute she moved in next door to me.

Chapter Twenty-seven

Isabella

"I'm gonna miss you guys so much," I tell my sisters as we embrace. We stay like that, holding onto each other for a full minute before the airport intercom announces my flight is now boarding.

Lily is ugly crying, but Rosa is putting on a brave face for all of us. Her eyes are glossy with the tears she's trying so hard to hold back.

"FaceTime us every day, okay?" Rosa says, her chin beginning to quiver.

"More than once a day!" Lily says, making us laugh.

Papa, who's been standing off to the side, letting us have our moment, comes forward and pulls me into his arms. He kisses the top of my head. Then he whispers, "Give Mama some time. She's stubborn."

"I know," I whisper back, burying my face in his chest. His flannel shirt smells faintly of fajitas, which is surprisingly soothing. Papa's arms are familiar and comforting, and I'm glad he's here to see me off. Even if my mother refused to come.

But these aren't the arms I want to find refuge in. I wish more than anything David was here so I could throw my arms around his neck and give him a long, passionate kiss goodbye.

Unfortunately, he's taking this three-week-break thing very seriously. I haven't heard a word from him in five days. Even when my sisters and I were next door packing up the house and hauling everything off to storage.

I already miss him so much.

And Mo. I hate leaving him behind too, but I know my sisters will take good care of him.

With one more hug for my father and my sisters, I walk to the security checkpoint, pausing to wave to my family one last time.

Thirty minutes later, I'm seated on the plane and check my phone before putting it on airplane mode.

I have one missed text and the name on the screen makes my heart come to life with little flutters of happiness.

David: Enjoy the first day of your grand adventure. I miss you already.

My eyes mist over with happy tears and I grin so big the spill over onto my cheeks.

Isabella: I miss you too.

I wake up late the next afternoon in my hotel room in Venice... Yes, afternoon. Jet lag is intense.

The new Monaco Hotel location is gorgeous. The style of the architecture was inspired by the Doge's Palace in St. Mark's Square, and the intricate details fit here in Venice so well. Although the room I'm staying in isn't a luxury suite like the one I toured in Kansas City, it's still beautiful and has a large window and balcony with a great view of the Adriatic Sea. The first thing I did when I got in early this morning was open the windows to let the ocean breeze in. The white gauzy curtains blow in the wind, making the room look like a dream. I sat on the balcony and watched the gondolas row by for a while, but I was so tired I could hardly stay awake.

The queen-sized bed is adorned with the same fluffy, white linens as the room I saw back in the states and it's just as comfortable as it looks. Like sleeping on a marshmallow. This room is much smaller, partially due to the fact that there's just a lot less space in Europe. But it's so cozy and romantic.

Which, of course, just makes me wish David was here. Sharing a tent with him was fun, but what would it be like to wake up next to him in this luxurious bed?

I can picture him asleep here, with the down comforter over his lower half and his chest exposed. The smattering of his dark chest hair contrasting with the white bedding. His glasses and night guard case neatly arranged on the nightstand beside him. And one arm thrown over his eyes like he so often did in his sleep in Peru. I smile at the bed before realizing this is all a stupid daydream, and he's not really here.

Glancing at the little white desk across from the bed where I set my laptop and new camera this morning, I decide to finish the article I began a few days ago. I calculate that I have three hours before the Monaco Hotel Gala tonight... just enough time to put my final touches on my "Midwest Food and Entertainment" article before I get dolled up for the party.

I had the idea to pay homage to my home state the day after my fight with Mama. The first place listed in my article of the top ten places to eat is Abuela's Restaurant. Of course, I don't draw attention to the fact that it's my family's restaurant, wanting to keep a piece of anonymity and also respect my family's privacy. I could've written an entire article about Abuela's alone with all of the photos I've taken of the staff, food, and decor. But I keep it simple.

After an hour of editing and making sure the article is perfect, I set it to appear on Isa's Itinerary first thing in the morning.

I spend the rest of my time getting ready for the semi-formal gala celebrating Monaco's 100th location. I ordered a dress on Amazon before I left the States, knowing I wouldn't have time to find a dress once I arrived here. The pink tiered, floor length dress drapes over my body perfectly. I love how it's flowy and moves with me, swishing around my feet when I walk. The dress is loose-fitting but shows off my tanned arms with two spaghetti straps that tie at my shoulders. Each tier of the dress is a different color of pink, creating an ombré effect.

Keeping my hair simple, since my dress has a wow factor on its own, I part it down the center and sweep it back into a low, braided chignon. Adding shimmery lotion to my skin and some large gold hoop earrings, my look is complete. I have just enough time to set up my tripod and new Nikon camera and take some photos for my website before I head downstairs.

I grab my small gold clutch bag before opening the hotel room door and stepping out into the narrow hallway when I see Bridget exiting her room across the hall.

She looks up and her eyes widen. "That dress is amazing!" Bridget tells me, making a circular motion with her index finger so I'll do a spin for her.

I oblige and twirl around, making my dress fan out at the bottom then twist around my ankles.

"You have to tell me where you got it," she says, her mouth agape as she studies the tiers of my dress.

I giggle. "Uh, it was like twenty dollars on Amazon."

Bridget gasps. "You're kidding!" She smooths her own sleek dress with one hand. "This boring old thing cost me nearly a grand."

My eyebrows raise. I can't imagine spending that much on a dress. "Well, you look gorgeous," I say as we begin walking toward the stairs. Bridget always looks stunning and classy. She has this simple yet sophisticated style that exudes good taste and money.

"Thank you." She winks before grabbing onto the railing and heading down the steps on her sky-high stilettos.

The elevator is minuscule, so despite our footwear, stairs are the easy choice.

We make it to the bottom of the stairs without tripping, and Bridget blows out a breath of relief. "I have so many people to introduce you to tonight!"

My heart speeds up, knowing all the bigwigs are here.

"Don't worry, they'll adore you." She gives me an endearing look then loops her arm through mine. "We'll stick together tonight, there's no need to be intimidated."

Bridget guides us through two large glass doors and onto a large terrace that's right on the water and decorated with thousands of fresh flowers. Bridget waves to someone she knows then tugs me over toward a server carrying a tray of colorful cocktails. She releases my arm so she can grab two cocktails and hands me one.

"For the nerves." She smiles and raises her glass before taking a sip.

Looking around the terrace, I instantly feel overwhelmed. The gentlemen are all wearing suits that look really expensive and perfectly tailored, and the ladies are dressed up in various cocktail dresses. The breeze coming off the water is cool, but my nerves are keeping me warm. I tip my glass up and finish my drink. It tastes so sweet and syrupy, I can barely detect a hint of alcohol. Basically, this cocktail is dangerous and I need to pace myself.

Bridget tugs on my elbow. "Oh! There's Dante Vergara, Monaco Hotel's CEO."

I focus my gaze where Bridget is looking and see an older but handsome man with dark hair and tanned skin. By his name I'm assuming he's Italian. He's surrounded by three younger men who look enough like him to be his sons, and they all have lovely dates with them.

One of the younger men in the group looks over and makes eye contact with me. He looks familiar. He turns to the blonde woman next to him and nudges her. She looks over at me, and my eyes widen in surprise.

I grin and rush towards Anthony and Hannah, who I haven't seen since leaving Peru.

"Isabella? Oh my gosh!" Hannah yells from halfway across the room, drawing everyone's attention to us.

I'm so excited to see her, my nerves are gone and we run to each other, squealing like teenagers. "Hannah!" I pull her into my arms as soon as we reach each other.

Anthony is behind her, grinning at us but also looking mildly embarrassed by our antics. Once his wife releases me, he steps forward and hugs me. "Great to see you, Isabella!"

"What are you guys doing here?" I ask, but before either of them can answer, the group they were with surrounds us.

The older gentleman, who looks like a slightly older version of Anthony and the other two young men in the group, extends his hand to me. "I don't believe we've met. I'm Anthony's father," He introduces himself in a smooth Italian accent. "This is my wife, Dominique."

A lovely woman steps forward and kisses both of my cheeks. "Welcome to Vicenza." When she pulls back, I get a better look at her beautiful face. She has faint smile lines indicating she's around the same age as her husband, but her dark hair tumbles around her slim shoulders in a cascade of shiny curls. Her dress is fitted to her figure and the champagne color of the silk brings out her olive complexion.

Bridget appears at my side. "Mr. Vergara, I meant to introduce you to Isabella, but your son beat me to it," she says in a teasing tone.

Anthony and Hannah laugh, but Mr. Vergara looks slightly confused. "Wait," he starts. "You're the Isabella behind Isa's Itinerary?"

I nod.

"But, how do you know my son and daughter-in-law?" he asks, huffing out a laugh.

Anthony interjects. "We had the pleasure of traveling with Isabella in Peru."

"Ahhhh," his father hums and smiles at him. "Well, it's wonderful to finally meet you. Bridget has been singing your praises."

Hannah pushes the two other young men forward. "Isabella, these are my brothers-in-law. Matteo," She pats the slightly shorter one on the shoulder. "And Salvador." She gestures to the taller one.

Matteo shakes my hand with a firm, business-like handshake, but Salvador bends and presses a kiss to my hand.

"Lovely to meet you. Save me a dance later?" he asks in a smooth Italian accent.

"Oh, ha. Sure," I reply, feeling my face heat as he looks at me with those intense, dark eyes.

Hannah tugs me away from him. "Alright, us ladies need to go to the powder room." She practically drags me across the terrace. I have no idea how she walks so fast in her form-hugging blue pantsuit and insanely tall, spikey heels.

Bridget gives me a concerned look, like she's telling me to blink twice if I'm okay. I smile at her so she knows I'm not being dragged against my will. We head back through the large glass doors and across the white marble lobby. Hannah pushes me inside the women's bathroom, checks all the stalls quickly before walking back over to the door and locking it.

"Oh my gosh, girl! What are you doing here?" Her perfect posture and graceful movements relax into the laid back girl I met in Peru. She kicks off her heels and slumps down onto the large pink ottoman at the center of the bathroom.

"Monaco Hotels is my newest sponsor. Bridget reached out to me after finding my website," I tell her and then take a seat next to her. "It's been a whirlwind, but now I'm able to travel and write full time."

"Congratulations! That's amazing! My in-laws seem a little stuffy, but they're actually super nice. Oh, and don't let Sal bug you, he's just a harmless flirt."

She gasps as if just remembering something. "Oh, my gosh! What happened with you and David?"

I release a heavy sigh and allow myself to fall back and sink into the plush ottoman. "When we got back, he took me on an official date, it was perfect."

She lays down next to me, like we're just two girls chatting at a slumber party. "Until you had to leave?"

"Exactly." I stare up at the ceiling that's painted in a Leonardo da Vinci style with clouds and cherubs. "I wanted to try long distance, and he didn't think it would work... so we're taking a break to think about things."

She groans. "Like a Ross and Rachel break?"

I laugh. "That's exactly what I asked him. He assured me it wasn't a Ross and Rachel break. Just some time apart so we can really think about *us*."

"I'm sorry," she says, wrinkling her nose. "Why doesn't he just travel with you?"

"He's a creature of comfort... he loves his house and his work. He's also really close with his family." A small smile tugs at one corner of my lips, remembering the family barbecue. "Their family gets together every Sunday for dinner."

Hannah gives me puppy-dog eyes. "Stop it, that's adorable." She sits up on the ottoman, looking thoughtful. "David's a smart man. If he wants to be with you, he'll figure out a way to make this work."

"I really hope so," I say with a dreamy sigh, wondering for the millionth time if I should've stayed in Kansas to be with him.

Propping myself up on both elbows, I narrow my eyes at her. "But enough about me... how about you leaving out the detail that you're married to the heir of a hotel empire?"

She throws her head back and laughs. "Technically, Matteo is the 'heir'" She says *heir* in air quotes. "Since he's the oldest. Then Anthony, then Salvador."

She sits all the way up and folds one leg up under herself. "Also, it doesn't really come up in casual conversation."

"True," I concede. "I thought you guys lived in Northern California?"

She grimaces. "We do, part of the time. That's our winter home. Anthony travels a lot for Monaco business. I go with him most of the time… but now that there's a baby on the way…"

I squeal and pull her into another hug. "A Machu Picchu baby!"

"Thank goodness you shared a tent with David instead of me." She giggles.

We hear a tap on the door and know that's our cue to unlock the door. Hannah stands up from the ottoman and smothers her sleek blonde hair down and slides her heels back on then unlocks the door.

A middle-aged woman in a short, black dress shoves her way past us, lecturing us in Italian. Hannah smiles at her and says something back to her in perfect Italian but the woman remains angry.

"Yikes," Hannah mutters under her breath as she closes the door behind us.

I follow her back to the terrace and grab another drink. Hannah asks the waiter for water, being newly pregnant and all.

"So what exactly does Anthony do?" I ask in a hushed voice.

"He oversees the Napa Valley and San Francisco locations." She spots her husband across the terrace and the moment he sees her his whole face lights up.

I was never one of those little girls who dreamt of her wedding. All I ever wanted was to travel the world and let my free spirit run rampant. And I still want that... but what do you do when your soul wants to sail and your heart wants to be anchored to another person? Someone to experience all of this adventure *with* me. Disney really needs to make a Moana 2, I need answers.

There's this longing in my heart for David to be here, looking at me the way Anthony looks at Hannah.

If David doesn't want to give this a chance, will I ever feel this way about another man? In twenty-eight years, David is the only one who made my heart feel like it might fly right out of my chest.

Salvador is standing next to Anthony and they both walk toward us. Well, Anthony walks... Salvador swaggers. He's the epitome of smooth. I nearly laugh out loud when I realize that Salvador Vergara is the Italian Brooks Windell.

As Salvador and Anthony draw closer to us, Salvador smiles then holds his hand out to me once he's right in front of me. "How about a dance?"

I have to withhold a laugh at how easy this must usually be for him. But not only does he look much younger than me, probably Lily's age, but sexy and flirtatious aren't my type. I'm into more serious, calculated sexiness... dark-rimmed glasses and a brain that works like a calculator helps too.

"Sure," I say with a smile, placing my hand in his and allowing him to guide me off to the side of the terrace where the dance floor is located.

There's a large pergola above the area filled with dancing couples. Lanterns are burning around the outdoor space, brightening the area with romantic light.

The DJ is playing an upbeat song and the dancers are laughing and having fun. Salvador begins to dance and I sway to the beat of the music. He places a hand on my waist, but keeps an appropriate distance between us, which I appreciate.

Sal asks me a few questions about myself, having to yell over the music. We end up chatting the whole time we're dancing, laughing and having a good time together. I'm not attracted to him at all. He seems like a little brother... a really tall one. Maybe I should give him Lily's number.

But even if I was dancing with someone my own age, or any of the attractive and well dressed men on the terrace—men that are most likely successful and have really cool accents—none of them could make my heart flutter the way David does.

And I'm positive none of them could make me want to lose my mind and fill their yard with plastic flamingos and cement geese.

Chapter Twenty-eight

David

Day six of the break: my yard looks boring without flamingos.

Day seven of the break: food has lost its taste... the sun has lost its warmth.

Day eight of the break: my house is lonely, I'm considering getting a cat.

Day nine of the break: I met with a client today and he told me I look like a love-sick puppy.

Day ten of the break: I can't live without Isabella Romero.

Closing my stupid, pointless journal, I prop my elbows on the dining table where I'm sitting and thrust my hands into my hair, grabbing it with my fingers and not caring if I rip it all out. I'm officially going mad.

With a groan, I swipe my phone off the table and send a text to the family group chat.

Windell family group chat:

David: Does anyone know a good real estate agent? The one I use only deals with commercial properties.

Madden: What do you need a realtor for?

Brooks: Finally. He's going after his woman! *gif of Ross from Friends yelling, *we were on a break.**

Sophie: Oh my gosh! You're going after Isa?? *gif of Monica, Rachel, and Phoebe from Friends jumping up and down and squealing*

Mom: Does anyone know if the *Find My Friends* app works internationally??

Dad: I know a great realtor, I'll forward his number. Heading into surgery now, please stop texting.

Dad texts me the number. I stand and dial it right away, walking to the large window in my front room as it rings.

"Hello, this is Ken Kase," a deep voice answers.

"My name is David Windell. My father, Ted, gave me your number. I need to put my house on the market." I look over at Isa's now empty house and feel an emptiness inside of myself. This house I loved so much when I bought it now feels pointless without her living next door.

"I can help you with that, when can we meet?" I hear a rustling of papers in the background as if he's making notes.

"Do you have any time today?"

There's a pause before he responds, "I can make time."

We agree on a time for him to stop by my home this afternoon and then say our goodbyes.

Next item on my list: stop at Abuela's and have a chat with Isa's father, then call all of my finance clients and let them know I'm moving to a different time zone.

Chapter Twenty-nine

Isabella

I've been in Italy for five days now and have explored most of Venice. The day after the gala, I had lunch with Anthony and Hannah before they left to head back to the States, then spent the rest of the day exploring the Peggy Guggenheim art collection. My third day here, I took a boat out to Murano Island for a tour of a glass factory, and then yesterday I spent most of the day writing, looking through the photos I've taken so far, and then relaxing at the hotel's spa.

Today, I'm just taking my time to meander around Venice. It's such a fun city to explore because you can walk the whole loop in a day and it's small enough you can't really get lost.

Wanting to visit and photograph as many restaurants and shops as possible while I'm here, I spread out my meals into tiny snacks at several different locations. Including the cutest gelato stand with a red and white striped canopy, where I just had the most delicious pistachio gelato of my existence.

I brought my camera and tripod with me to get some more photos. I want to have enough content for my website until I travel to my next destination. Right next to the gelato stand, there's a lovely little stone bridge. I instantly see it as the perfect creative opportunity and set up my camera equipment in front of the tiny bridge. It's such a cute spot to get a photo of the blue water flowing between the buildings.

I wore white linen pants today with a camel colored body suit. I wanted to be pretty neutral so in photos the attention stays mostly on the colorful buildings surrounding me. The city is so beautiful; I knew it would be easy to get artistic photos. It's still a little awkward posing in front of my camera with so many people around, but it's a big part of my job and I need to get comfortable with it.

Turning on the Bluetooth camera remote, I hurry toward the bridge to capture a few different poses. In one I face away from the camera, like I'm looking off in the distance. Next I put on my sunglasses, sent to me by a new sponsor, and snap a few more so my readers can see them. I even have a discount code from the company to share.

With the stone bridges, colorful architecture and old-world charm, Venice is unmistakably a city of romance. I can't imagine a more perfect place for a honeymoon. It actually reminds me a bit of the steakhouse David took me to.

I've decided one of the articles I'll write will be "Why You Should Honeymoon in Venice." Even though I haven't been on a honeymoon, I can use my imagination. And I honestly don't think it'll be difficult to convince my readers that Venice is one of the most romantic cities to honeymoon in.

If David were here, I could stage some incredibly romantic photos of the two of us to really sell it. I sigh and put my camera and tripod away in my backpack.

My cell phone rings from the small pocket in the front of my backpack and I pull it out to see Mama's face on the screen. My heart skips a beat at the sight of her face. I close my eyes and remind myself it's probably Papa calling from her phone.

I answer the call and the FaceTime screen pops up, and it actually really is Mama.

"Mama? Hey," I say awkwardly before grabbing my backpack and walking over to a bench next to the bridge to sit down.

"Bella," She starts and then glances away from the camera, as if unsure what to say. When she looks back toward the camera again, I see the red around her eyes like she's either been crying, or hasn't been sleeping well. "How are you?"

I give her a hesitant smile. "Pretty good. Venice is lovely."

She inhales a deep breath and blows it out slowly. "Papa showed me your website. Your article featuring Abuela's was wonderful.."

My eyes widen before I school my features, not wanting her to see how surprised I am that she read one of my articles. "Thank you for reading it, I'm glad you liked it."

"Honestly, I hadn't ever looked at your website before your Papa made me sit down and read it." She looks down and shakes her head, almost like she's reprimanding herself. "You're a very talented writer."

I'm unable to disguise my shock this time. "Thank you, Mama. It means so much to me to hear you say that."

"Also, you were right about Rosa's leadership skills. Since you left we put her in charge of the scheduling and she's doing great."

I smile, picturing how happy my sister must be. She's been wanting a chance to prove herself for years. "That's awesome."

She huffs out a breathy laugh. "Papa says I've been too exhausted and stressed to think clearly... I think it's time to cut back my hours at Abuela's." Her mouth sets in a straight line, like the thought of cutting back will be difficult for her. "Who knows, maybe I'll do some traveling of my own... someday."

"You definitely should. Take some time to stop and smell the roses." I wink at the screen and she laughs. A sound I haven't heard in the past few years, and it brings so much joy to my heart. "I miss you all."

"We miss you too, Bella."

An awkward pause passes, I'm not sure what else to say, and it's obvious she's not either. The hurt we've caused each other can't be brushed away in one conversation... but this is a step in the right direction.

Mama tells me she needs to get back to work and we say our goodbyes. My heart has a lightness that I haven't felt in the past few months. I love my parents, and my relationship with them is important to me. Mama's phone call makes me hopeful that things could be mended between us in the future.

That evening, I'm having dinner at the Monaco Café attached to the hotel. I made sure to dress warm so I could eat outside by the water. I'm dressed down in black leggings and a white v-neck tee paired with a cardigan that drapes all the way down to my calves. The café is pretty empty tonight and I'm the only one seated outside. I pull my legs into my arms and rest my feet on the chair, hugging my knees to my chest.

Soft Italian music plays in the background as I look out onto the water, which is dark except for the reflection of the outdoor lights and lanterns. I sip on my glass of red wine while I zone out looking out at the darkness, and remember the night David and I sat on a mountain top looking at the stars. A feeling of loneliness fills me, making my eyes become wet with tears.

I've traveled alone for years, and have never felt homesick or lonely. But tonight, the reflected light rippling in the dark water seems to mirror my soul.

Deep down, I know I feel this way because I miss David. It's like I found the missing piece of my puzzle and now everything seems a little off without it.

I don't know how and I don't know when... but I fell in love with him and now I'm alone.

The deep, rumbling sound of a man clearing his throat interrupts my thoughts. I sigh, knowing it's probably the café manager wanting to lock up for the night, but going back to my hotel room seems even more lonely than sitting here at this table.

Leaving my glass of wine behind, I stand from the wrought iron table. But the man standing there stops me in my tracks.

The music in the background and the sound of the water still, and all I can hear is the thumping of my heart.

"Isa," David whispers, releasing his grasp on the handle of his suitcase.

I can't even speak, I'm so shocked at the sight of him, here in Italy. The last person I was expecting to see, but the one person I've wanted here the most.

Tears roll down my face and I run to him. He opens his arms and I jump into them, throwing my arms around his neck and wrapping my legs around his waist.

His hands grab my thighs to hold me there, and I rest my lips against his neck, savoring the masculine scent that I've missed so much. We stay like that for a full minute before he releases his hold on me.

I drop back down, my feet meeting the floor. "David—"

He cuts me off with a kiss that's hungry, hard, desperate. A kiss that tells me he's been just as lost without me as I have him. A kiss that sears my skin, warming me from my lips to my toes, and all throughout my body.

When he pulls back, his eyes are filled with tears just like mine, and he kisses me once more.

I pull away just enough to catch my breath. Both of our chests are heaving. He rests his forehead against mine as if to calm himself after the intensity of seeing me again.

"I was an idiot," he says, finally. "I'm in love with you."

His eyes are full of passion and shining with tears, which makes my own tears come even quicker. "Oh David, I love you too." I laugh in spite of the emotion in my voice. "So you're willing to make this long distance thing work?"

He smirks. "No, absolutely not."

My heart stops, and I try to pull back but his hands tighten around my waist.

"I can't be away from you," he says before dropping down on one knee.

My hands fly up to cup over my mouth as I gasp in shock. We've been on *one* official date, have never called each other boyfriend or girlfriend, and are supposed to be on a break... And yet here he is, down on one knee, looking at me like I'm his entire universe and pulling a box out of his pants pocket. The red, velvet box looks like an antique. And when he opens it, I recognize my Abuela's ring.

"Isabella Romero, you have driven me to the brink of madness—"

I huff out a sigh of annoyance. "Really?"

The corner of his lips twitch in amusement. "Would you just let me finish?"

"Okay fine."

"Anyway, as I was saying... You've driven me to the brink of madness, and turned my perfectly organized, scrupulously scheduled, orderly life... completely upside down." He takes my left hand in his. "But oddly enough, everything looks better upside down... and my world is utterly boring without you in it. Will you marry me?"

Despite the short timeline of our romantic relationship, I don't have a single doubt in my mind that I can happily spend forever with this man.

"Absolutely." I bend at the waist and put both of my hands on his sculpted cheeks, then plant a kiss on his lips.

When I hear a meow, I pull back, and my jaw nearly drops all the way to the floor. "Mo?"

David grins. "Mo also wants to become a Windell."

He stands and turns, and I notice his large backpack for the first time. The backpack is a hard dome made of clear plastic and Mo is inside.

My eyes fill with tears again, and my hands come up to cover my face. David's arms wrap around me and he kisses the top of my head.

"Does the Monaco Hotel have pet-friendly rooms?"

I burst into laughter at his question, and his cat backpack, and the fact that this orderly man flew halfway across the world with a cat without even checking to see if the hotel had accommodations for pets.

David begins laughing too, then stops and pulls away slightly. "I forgot to put the ring on your finger."

"Oh yeah!" I splay my left hand out in front of him and he slides the familiar antique ring onto my finger. "How on earth did you get my Abuela's ring?"

He arches an eyebrow. "I asked your father for your hand and he gave me the ring. If you don't want this one, we can pick out a different one."

"No, this ring is perfect." I look at my hand, admiring the sparkly round diamond set in between two smaller ones, surrounded by an intricate gold band. "Wait, you talked to my father?"

"Of course I did," he says in a slightly offended tone, like asking my father's permission was a given. "I had to promise to attend Mass with the family whenever we're in Kansas, but he gave his blessing."

Picturing Papa and David chatting and my father bargaining with him to come to Mass puts a huge grin on my face.

Chapter Thirty

David

Early the following morning, I wake up from the small pullout sofa in Isa's room. It was too late when I arrived to bother booking a separate room, and I was also too exhausted. Isa is still sleeping peacefully in the bed, surrounded by white fluffy pillows and blankets. She's asleep on her back with her hair fanned out on the pillow behind her. Her left hand is resting against her clavicle, and the engagement ring sparkles in the morning sunlight coming in through the large window. Mo is curled up on her feet.

Call me old-fashioned, but I didn't want to sleep in the same bed until we're married... and if she agrees with my plan, we'll be able to share a bed soon enough. However, laying down next to her for a moment couldn't hurt.

Careful not to wake her, I slide under the covers next to her and wrap an arm around her waist. Oh yes, I could definitely get used to waking up like this every morning. Mo purrs loudly and moves from her feet to mine.

"Traitor," she whispers to the beast at the foot of the bed. He ignores her and snuggles in between my legs.

Her eyes flicker open and she leans into my side. "Good morning, future husband," she says, her face now right in front of mine. A sleepy smile appears on her lovely face and I smile back.

"Your breath smells horrible," I say back, in the sexiest voice I can muster without laughing.

She slaps me on the chest and rolls away from me. I scoot closer and pull her close again. She doesn't bother trying to escape. I savor the moment of her in my arms and rest my chin on her shoulder.

"So… we should talk about our wedding," I say, knowing it will get her attention. "I'd like to get married soon."

She unwraps my arms from her waist and sits up, leaning back against the tufted headboard. "Like… how soon?"

"How about tomorrow?"

Isa laughs for a moment before realizing I'm not joking. She studies my serious expression for a moment before her eyebrows shoot up. "You can't be serious. Our families wouldn't even be able to come."

I grimace, but it quickly forms into a smile. "Actually, our families are flying to Venice tomorrow." I sit up and look earnestly into my eyes. "I flew them out to celebrate our engagement. So we could just have the wedding when they're here… but it's completely up to you—"

"Yes! Let's get married tomorrow," she says with a little squeal. I arch a brow, silently asking if she's sure. "David, I've never dreamt of a big, perfect wedding. As long as our families are there, that's all I care about."

We grin at each other for a moment before I speak again, "Get dressed. We have a wedding to plan."

She grabs my hand to stop me from flying off the bed to get ready. "David, are you sure about this? I know you like to have things planned out, with all the details lined up."

I sit back down on the edge of the bed and pull her onto my lap. "Believe it or not, I've taken some risks in business... but only when I'm absolutely sure the investment will be worth it in the end. And Isa, I've never been more confident in an investment in my life than this one."

She jumps out of my lap and stands next to the bed, her eyes alight with excitement. "Okay, then let's do this."

We take the stairs down to the lobby, not even sure where to start with this whole wedding thing. A man around my dad's age, dressed in an expensive Italian suit—one I'm quite jealous of—spots Isa and smiles, walking toward us with the gait only a powerful man would have.

"Isabella! How are you enjoying the hotel?" he asks in an Italian accent that would make any woman swoon... okay *I* may have even swooned a little.

"Mr. Vergara, I didn't know you were still in Venice." She lets go of my hand and places it on my arm. "This is my.... fiancé, David."

He shakes my hand. “Fiancé?”

I smile and let go of his hand. “As of last night, yes,” I tell him proudly.

He claps his hands together. “Magnifico! Congratulations.”

“Get this,” Isa says to me. “This is Anthony’s father. Anthony from Peru.”

“You’re kidding.” My voice sounds as bewildered as I feel. “What a small world.”

“Yes, indeed,” Mr. Vergara agrees.

“Anthony and Hannah were at the celebration gala. I could hardly believe it.”

I chuckle. “I bet. What are the chances.”

A woman with long, dark hair appears in the lobby and looks around as if looking for someone. When she spots Mr. Vergara, her demeanor softens and she walks toward us.

Mr. Vergara hears the sound of her heels clacking against the marble and turns to look over his shoulder. “Amore! Come meet Isabella’s fiancé, David. This is my wife, Dominique.”

He places a hand on her back and she leans forward to kiss both of my cheeks. She smells of expensive perfume, but it’s not unpleasant.

“They just got engaged last night,” He tells her.

“How wonderful!” she says in an equally charming accent to that of her husband. “When’s the wedding?”

Mr. Vergara’s head drops back as he laughs loudly, filling the lobby with his deep baritone laughter. “Darling, they just got engaged.” He looks at me and cups a hand over his mouth like he's telling me a secret. "Women, always in a rush."

I chuckle and his wife gives him an annoyed look. "Actually, we'd like to get married tomorrow."

Both of their eyebrows shoot up to their hairlines.

Isa giggles next to me, leaning her head on my shoulder. "Why wait? When you know, you know, right?"

Dominique sighs dreamily. She looks up at her husband and a conspiratorial glance passes between them.

"You should get married here, on the terrace!" She suggests. "I know a priest in town that could perform the marriage. And a dress shop." Her voice raises as she speaks, like she can't contain her excitement. "Oh, please let me help you!"

"Of course! I need all the help I can get," Isa tells her.

"The photographer we used for the gala is still in town I believe. Shall I contact him and see if he's available tomorrow?" Mr. Vergara asks.

I huff out a laugh. "Wow, thank goodness we ran into you two. We had no idea what we were doing."

Dominique pulls out her phone and types away on it with her long, pointy fingernails. "Alright, I've started a list. I'll take Isabella to the dress shop and you two track down the photographer?" She briefly looks up from her phone to give her husband a pointed glance.

"Got it," He reassures her.

She finishes her typing and walks to Isa's side and loops an arm through hers. "Let's go mon chéri. We have a dress to find."

Dominique walks quickly, a woman on a mission. Isa glances back at me, looking half terrified of what she's gotten herself into. I smile and shrug one shoulder.

"I'll have my secretary call the photographer. What else do we need?" Mr. Vergara taps his chin.

"I'll probably need one of those Italian suits," I tell him, eyeing his suit and shoes.

"Ah, an eye for a good suit. A man after my own heart." He slaps me on the back. "I'll take care of it. Follow me."

The sun has gone down by the time Isa and I reunite after spending the day prepping for the wedding. I meet Isa at a restaurant Mr. Vergara, who insisted I call him Dante, recommended.

The Vergaras pulled a million strings for us today... but I'm most excited about my custom Italian suit and loafers, which will be delivered tomorrow. Although I'd marry Isa in anything, or nothing, whatever she wanted.

Our families are flying across the world as we speak, having no idea they'll be attending our wedding tomorrow and not an engagement party.

Walking into the quaint Italian restaurant, I'm a little surprised it's nothing grand or fancy, seeing as it was recommended by Dante. But he insisted it's the best food in the city, so I'll take his word for it.

I find Isa already seated. She smiles at me happily, but her eyes look tired. "Did you survive your day with Dominique?" I ask before leaning down and kissing her.

She laughs and it turns into a yawn. "Barely. Dominique could outshop a Beverly Hills socialite."

I take my seat across from her, my shoulders shaking from trying to hold in my laughter. "Did you find a dress?"

Her eyes brighten. "I did, it's perfect. You're going to die when you see it."

"Is it easy to take off?"

Her jaw drops in mock offense. "David Windell, you saucy little minx!"

We laugh until the waiter interrupts to take our order. We both request the lasagna, per Dante's insistence, and a bottle of red wine. The waiter leaves to put our order in and once he's gone, I stretch my arms across the table and take Isa's hands in mine.

"So, where are we going to purchase a flat?"

She bites her bottom lip. "Before you got here, I was going back and forth between Edinburgh and London."

"London. Definitely London," I say without hesitation.

She wrinkles her nose. "What's wrong with Edinburgh?"

"I have a disturbing feeling there's not a chance we could live in Scotland and you wouldn't make me wear a kilt at *least* once."

She laughs so hard she snorts. "You're absolutely right. But I think you'd look great in a kilt."

"I think I'm more of a high-tea kind of guy," I say dryly. She twists her lips but then finally nods her agreement.

"Should we just get a studio?" she asks before the waiter comes back with garlic bread and our bottle of wine. He carefully pours us each a glass and then heads back toward the kitchen again.

I take a sip of wine. "How about a two bedroom? I can set up an office in one of them. I want to travel with you as much as possible, but sometimes I'll need to stay behind and work."

"Okay, that makes sense." She grabs a breadstick and tears off a piece. "Traveling without you will be a little sad... but knowing you're in London waiting for me and not all the way back in Kansas makes it better." She grins and pops the bread into her mouth, chews and swallows it. "You know, this is all so adventurous of you. I never thought you'd leave your home."

I look into her eyes fervently, so she knows what I'm about to say is serious. She stills and meets my gaze. "Isa, you're my home now. You've helped me discover that there's value in spontaneity... in fact, I think it's been good for me."

Chapter Thirty-one

Isabella

The next morning, I wake up in the honeymoon suite that the Vergaras upgraded us to. David stayed in the smaller room with Mo and will join me here tonight after our nuptials.

The thought of sleeping in the same bed with him, not just next to him in a tent… makes goosebumps appear all over my skin.

While I'm getting dressed to meet our families for breakfast, I glance at my lace-embellished slip-dress hanging in the bathroom, which makes me positively giddy. I can't believe how everything just fell into place… In a few hours, I'll be David's wife.

David should be back from the airport soon with our families in tow and I'm meeting them at the hotel café so we can tell them about our impromptu wedding.

Is it considered eloping if your families are there? I'm not sure what constitutes an elopement over a last-minute wedding. But it doesn't really matter.

I'm taking a little longer than normal on my hair and makeup so I look nice in wedding photos, but I just threw on some leggings and a flowy button down top for breakfast since I'll change into my dress later.

After making my way downstairs, I take a detour outside to the trellis. Wrought iron chairs from the café make a few small rows for our families and leave an opening for an aisle. My heart skips inside my chest as I imagine walking down the aisle toward David. No decorations were needed for the trellis since it's covered with vines and flowering plants already. The Adriatic Sea completes the backdrop perfectly.

I walk to the other end of the trellis that leads inside the café and find the long table we reserved. A minute later, David walks into the café followed by our whole families… Well, everyone but Mama.

He shares a secret smile with me before my sisters run and attack me with hugs and kisses.

"We're so happy for you!" Lily squeals into my ear as she hugs me, nearly causing my eardrum to rupture.

"Quit hogging her!" Rosa teases as she pushes Lily away so she can hug me too. "Congratulations, Bella."

"Thank you," I tell them before I'm pulled into another hug, this time by Papa. He holds me tight for a moment before whispering, "I'm sorry Mama didn't come."

"Me too," I say, pulling back to look at him. "Thank you for giving your blessing, Papa." I give him a kiss on the cheek and he grins.

"Honestly, you're so independent, I never dreamed a man would ask for my permission. He impressed me."

Pride fills my heart at his comment, loving that my father respects the man I'm marrying.

"Okay, let's see this ring!" Sophie says, coming toward me. Odette, and David's mom, Diane, join her and the three of them bombard me.

Diane grabs my left hand and gasps. "Oh it's gorgeous! Your grandmother had excellent taste."

Sophie nods in agreement. "It's stunning."

Odette tears up. "I'm so happy someone is finally marrying David."

Brooks sidles up next to me and gives me a big side-hug. "I can't *believe* someone is actually marrying David."

Drew appears next to Sophie, Samantha in his big arms and Penny right beside him. "Congratulations. David really is the best. Ignore Brooks."

Madden joins the circle. Oliver is asleep on his shoulder and Bradford is barely standing upright while sleepily clinging to his leg. "Drew's right. You couldn't have picked a better man, Isabella." He yawns.

Ted, David's dad, gives me a pat on the shoulder. "Congratulations to you both."

I feel warm arms wrap around my waist from behind and know it's David. He presses a kiss on the sensitive skin behind my ear and whispers, "Are you ready to tell them?"

A rush of nerves flutters through me, but I nod my answer.

David releases me and clears his throat to get everyone's attention. "Why don't you all have a seat? We have a bit of a surprise."

Penny jumps up and down. "Oh, I hope it's a gondola ride!"

Everyone chuckles at her comment as they each find a seat at the table. "Sorry, Pen. That's not it." Her shoulders slump in disappointment.

The table quiets down and waits for David to announce the surprise. "I know you all came here expecting to just celebrate our engagement... but our wedding is in..." He glances down at his watch. "two hours."

Audible gasps and mutterings fly around the table. "Two hours?" Ted asks, his eyes wide with shock. "But you *just* got engaged."

"Seriously?" Brooks crosses his arms over his chest in a pout. "This will be the first wedding ever where I haven't brought a date."

Madden, who's sitting next to him, whops him on the back of the head. "Would you shut up? Not everything is about you."

"Ow!" Brooks protests, then grabs Madden in a headlock.

Diane stands up from her seat, releasing an overly dramatic groan, and walks to stand behind them. She pulls them apart easily, which is impressive since she's so tiny. "Stop acting like children," she whisper-yells.

Papa looks on with concern, never having raised boys. Madden and Brooks shape up quickly after being chastised by Diane.

"Listen," David starts again. "We know this is happening fast. But neither of us care about a big, fancy wedding... and we're just ready to start our lives together."

Drew speaks up, "When you find the one your soul belongs to, it's impossible to wait." He smiles at Sophie. "So, let's get these two married."

"Agreed," Papa says, nodding his head in our direction.

Little Samantha starts crying for no apparent reason and her cousin, Bradford joins in. Drew hands her to Sophie and she rubs her back gently and makes a shushing sound.

Madden stands from his seat with a hesitant expression. "I don't want to be rude, but since the wedding is in two hours... do you mind if we skip breakfast and get some sleep instead?"

Odette yawns. "Yes, please."

Sophie grimaces, probably since the child in her arms won't stop crying. "That's probably not a bad idea."

David gives her an endearing glance. "Of course. Your rooms are already reserved and ready for you." He pulls a packet of key cards out of his pants pocket and hands them to their designated families.

The group disperses toward the stairs. "Meet back here at eleven," David calls after them and they grunt in response.

Once they're all gone, I wrap my arms around my fiancé's waist and look up at his ridiculously handsome face. "You think they'll be in better moods after their naps?"

He chuckles. "Hopefully. Jet lag is the worst."

Two hours pass quickly when your fiancé sends you to the spa for a mani-pedi to relax while he stays in the lobby making sure the priest and photographer arrive on time. When my nails are buffed and shined to perfection, I have just enough time to run up to the suite to touch up my makeup and slip my dress on.

The silky fabric flows over my body like it was made for me, even though I purchased it straight off the rack without any alterations. The nude colored slip dress dips down in front making a deep V shape, and the back is.... Well, backless. The nude silk has a cream colored overlay with a few lace details attached around the bodice and the hem of the skirt. It's sexy and simple.

I hear a knock and rush from the bathroom to the hotel door. I look through the peephole to make sure it's not David, I don't want him to see my dress until I'm walking down the aisle.

My sisters' faces come into view and I unlatch the door and open it quickly. They step inside the room, both wearing lovely dresses—courtesy of Dominique.

They gasp in unison as they take in my wedding dress. Rosa steps forward and kisses my cheek then hands me the bouquet of wildflowers the florist delivered to the lobby earlier. "You look beautiful, and more importantly... you look happy."

Lily kisses me next. "You're gorgeous."

"We practically had to wrestle the bouquet away from David... he wanted to come see you so badly. It was kind of adorable," Rosa says, shaking her head but smiling.

I laugh and ask them to help me with my hair. It's down and curled, but I swept the sides back in two braids, pulling on them until they looked loose and messy. "I just need these flowers pinned in." I point to the side table where half a dozen colorful, miniature roses sit in a vase.

"I can do that," Lily volunteers. I sit on the bed so she can reach the top of my head better. Before she starts with the flowers, she pulls a slip of paper out of the bodice of her dress and places it in my lap. I instantly recognize Mama's stationary. "Mama wanted me to give you this."

I read the note while Lily carefully places the flowers in my hair. Rosa sits next to me, her hand on my arm as I read.

Bella,

I'm sorry I'm not there to celebrate with you. I felt someone needed to stay back and take care of things at Abuela's. I know things between us aren't perfect, but please know that I love you, and I hope David knows how lucky he is to be yours.

-Mama

I choke back the tears that threaten to ruin my perfect makeup and grab my phone off the bed to text Mama.

Isabella: Thank you for the note, Mama. Wish you were here. I love you.

Lily finishes with my hair and gives me a final spritz of hairspray. "Perfect," she says when she's all done.

Rosa's phone pings with a text and she picks it up and smiles. "It's David. He says everything's ready for your grand entrance."

I inhale a deep breath and exhale it slowly before a wide grin takes over my face. I follow my sisters out of the room and down the stairs where my father is waiting to walk me down the aisle.

Chapter Thirty-two

David

I'm standing in front of the stone railing on the trellis, my family already seated and smiling now that they've had a nice long nap. Even the kids are in good spirits. Dante and Dominique Vergara are here as well; Dante kindly volunteered to translate for the priest.

I'm wearing my new Italian suit. It's an indigo blue color with a white, collared shirt underneath and a pale pink tie and matching pocket square. The suit pants are a modern cut, tapering at the ankles, which compliments the brown leather oxfords nicely.

I look pretty damn good. But I know there's no way I look better than my bride probably does. Even though this suit probably cost twice as much as her dress. Isa can wow me in a little pink bikini, in a baggy t-shirt, in athletic gear… I've seen it all and I've liked it all.

Isa's sisters appear at the French doors leading onto the trellis and make their way to their seats. I have to roll my lips together to keep from grinning like an idiot, knowing Isa and her father will appear next.

La Vie En Rose starts to play softly through the speakers and everyone looks at the French doors in anticipation.

Isa and her father walk through the doors. Her father is holding onto her arm tightly, his eyes alight with tears. Isa is looking at me with a grin so wide her cheeks must hurt. And I'm probably grinning just as big as she is.

I take this opportunity to appreciate the dress she chose and how it hugs her body in all the right places. It dips down enough in the front to be incredibly sexy, but not so low that it would make our families uncomfortable. Her bouquet is perfect for her, a colorful arrangement that cascades in all directions. It's wild and beautiful… just like the woman holding it.

When they're finally right in front of me, she leans over to kiss her father on the cheek and I see her hair has the same flowers as her bouquet. Her father tearfully takes his own seat and Isa hands her bouquet off to her sister, Rosa, so she can take my hands.

When she finally meets my gaze, I whisper, "Wow."

At least I thought I whispered it… but our families are laughing.

Dante comes up and stands next to me as the priest begins the ceremony, which is completely in Italian. Dante effortlessly translates, probably captivating all of the women in the room… except for Isa, whose attention is on me. Just the way I like it.

When it's time to exchange rings, I realize we completely forgot to purchase a ring for me. "I forgot to buy myself a ring," I whisper to Isa.

The priest looks between us with a confused expression.

Isa winks at me. "Don't worry, I've got you."

Isa's younger sister, Lily, comes walking down the aisle, and Mo is on a leash walking beside her. He's wearing a very dapper bow tie and looks absolutely miserable.

I chuckle and shake my head at the sight. Our families love the scene and are all laughing and snapping photos with their phones.

Lily and Mo finally make it to the front and, with a little coercion via cat treats, she bends to untie my ring and Isa's wedding band from Mo's collar and then hands them to us.

Lily then picks Mo up, then carries him off to her seat. The priest smiles and continues as we exchange our rings. Mine is a simple band made of dark gold, matching Isa's perfectly.

The priest exclaims something in Italian with a big smile and Dante translates that it's time to kiss the bride.

With one hand on her back, which I'm delighted is completely bare, and one hand at her nape, I dip her back and kiss her with all of the built up passion I felt when we were apart. And all of the relief I feel that we never have to be apart again.

Our families whoop and holler, making enough noise that you'd think our wedding had a hundred guests.

I bring Isa back up and surprise her by picking her up off the ground. A festive Italian song blares from the speakers and I start carrying her down the aisle. Our families continue cheering until they realize I'm not stopping. I've nearly reached the staircase with my bride before we hear Brooks yell, "You're not even going to eat lunch with us?"

"Nope!" I yell back.

Once we get to the narrow staircase, I set Isa down and we run up the stairs as fast as we can... with the exception of the several times we stopped to make out along the way.

Isa opens the door to our suite and when I see the bed, I squeeze my eyes shut in horror. "Did you do this?"

She stares at the bed and starts to giggle. The longer she looks at it, the harder she laughs.

"This had to have been Brooks... but when did he sneak away to do this??" I gesture toward the bad in annoyance with one hand. Isa doesn't answer because she's too busy laughing.

I begin removing the condoms-turned-balloons that are taped all over our bed, and then I tackle the flamingo and llama confetti.

My wife—wow, I love the sounds of that—finally calms down and places a hand on my arm, urging me to stop my cleaning. Closing my eyes and taking a deep breath, I slip my arms around her and force myself to forget the giant mess of confetti.

"Our life is going to be a constant adventure, isn't it?" I ask before running my lips along the side of her neck, the mess forgotten the instant my lips meet her skin.

"I sure hope so," she whispers back.

David

Six Months Later

"David, hurry! We're going to be late for our flight!" Isa calls from the kitchen in our two-bedroom flat in London.

The white walls are still mostly bare and our furniture is minimal with all the traveling we've been doing, but it's starting to feel like home. Mo runs into my office, his paws sliding all over the wood floor. He hops up on my desk, causing papers to scatter.

I glare at the behemoth cat, but he's not scared. He's figured out I'm a softie, deep down inside… very deep down.

After submitting all the correct paperwork online for Isa's self-employment taxes, I grab the papers off the floor and stack them back together.

Isa appears in the doorway and leans against it. "Who would've thought *you'd* be the one causing us to be late?"

I turn and open a drawer of the filing cabinet behind me and place the tax documents in the folder labeled *Isa's Itinerary.* Smiling to myself, I wonder why I bother with files anymore since my wife is now my only client. But the finances and tax preparations for her website and sponsorships are more than enough of a workload for me. Which is why I dropped all my other clients a few months after our wedding.

Turning back around, I walk toward her, allowing my eyes to slowly peruse her body. Navy leggings clinging to her curvy legs, a white athletic tank showing off her tanned shoulders, and hair in a messy bun so I can see that little spot on her neck, right under her earlobe, where she loves to be kissed.

I slip my arms around her waist. "I believe my punctuality is rubbing off on you."

She twists in my arms like she's trying to get away, but she's smiling and gives up quickly. "Our flight leaves in two hours, David."

"Actually, it leaves in one-hundred and twenty-nine minutes."

Her hands slide up my chest and rest right over my heart. "I'm just excited to see our families. So, are you finally done working?"

Leaning back, I quirk one eyebrow. "You mean... submitting *your* taxes?"

She grimaces. "Oh, is that what you've been doing in here all morning?"

I nod my head.

Isa leans in and trails kisses up my neck before whispering, "Have I told you lately how much I appreciate my CPA?"

"You haven't, as a matter of fact." I take a step back and cross my arms, waiting for her to express her undying love and appreciation for me.

Her mouth quirks into a smirk. "Not only is he extremely handsome but also very good at pantry organization and making labels."

I want to puff out my chest. I absolutely love it when she compliments my organization like this. But it's more fun to annoy her... so with a bored sigh, I check the watch on my wrist. "Alright, enough with the chitchat. We need to leave for the airport posthaste."

She grips the front of my button-down shirt in her fist when I attempt to brush past her, then pulls me toward her. Isa pops up onto her tippy-toes and kisses me. Not a brief peck... but a kiss with so much passion I'm tempted to hoist her over my shoulder and carry her back to the bedroom. Kansas be damned.

Tightening my hands around her waist, I slowly begin pushing her backward, down the short hallway. Isa bursts into laughter, ending our kiss.

"We are seriously going to miss our flight at this rate!" She ambles across the room, putting space between us.

Isa ignores my pouting, gives Mo one last pet, then grabs her backpack and turns toward the front door.

Groaning, I follow her. "Who would've thought my little travel writer would be so eager to go to... Kansas?"

I grab the handles of the suitcases and roll them toward the door.

"Definitely not me," she admits. "But we haven't gotten to hang out with our families as a married couple. And I'm excited to see Mama."

I smile at her before letting go of a suitcase to open the front door. Isa and her mother are getting along much better these days... having an ocean between them helps, I think. "I know. I'm excited to see everyone, too."

Isa follows me through the door with our carry-on bags in hand and closes the door to our flat behind her. We make our way toward the elevator, and once we're inside, she rummages around her backpack. "Where's my passport?" Her eyes snap up to meet mine. "Did you re-pack my bags again?"

"Guilty. The way you pack wastes so much space." I wrinkle my nose.

She shakes her head in dismay. "You keep me safe, and I keep you wild. Remember?"

"Yes, precisely."

"And that's why I replaced all of your underwear with ones that have my face on them."

My heart stops for a second, and I'm sure my eyes are about as wide as they can go. "You what?"

The elevator stops, and the door opens to the ground floor. Isa grins and steps off the elevator. Still speechless, I follow her. Surely she's joking.

"Don't worry, they're exceptional quality. I saw them on a social media ad. They had great reviews." She continues walking out onto the busy London sidewalk and lifts her arm to hail a taxi.

"A random ad?" My voice is coming out high-pitched and a little squeaky. "What about my Calvin Klein's?"

A white taxi pulls up and stops in front of us. The cab driver sees our luggage and pops the trunk before stepping out of the car and taking the luggage from Isa. She ducks inside the vehicle and I have to close my eyes for a beat to control my irritation. After loading the suitcases into the trunk, I walk around to the other side of the taxi and slide in next to my wife.

She places her small hand on top of mine, looking up at me through her lashes with those big, brown eyes. "I can't wait to see you in them."

The infuriating woman knows I can't stay annoyed with her when she looks at me like that. She's not playing fair.

Releasing a heavy sigh, I shrug off my irritation and slip an arm around her. "You really want to start the prank wars again?" My brain is already a flurry of ideas.

"Oh no," she says, pulling back slightly. "I don't like that calculating look on your face."

"I have no idea what you mean."

She locks her gaze with mine and we face off in a staring contest. Finally, she breaks the silence, "Just play nice, okay? Your Calvin Klein's are still in your dresser drawer... but all the undies in your suitcase have my face on them."

I continue staring at her with a blank expression.

"David, say something," she pleads.

“Fine,” I concede. “I’ll wear them, but when you least expect it… I’ll get you back.”

Isa giggles and leans against my shoulder. “I can’t wait.”

Acknowledgments

As always, one person alone does not complete a book.

Thank you to my wonderful editor, Amy Guan. Your ideas and input were invaluable to the completion of Check Mate! You turned my manuscript into an actual book.

To my amazing beta readers, Amanda from @my.bookish.heart, and Meredith from @abookandacupof-cocoa, you guys are awesome! Thank you for taking the time to read through my very early, very messy draft.

Thank you to the lovely Gigi Blume for doing a sensitivity read and helping me fine tune Isabella and her family!

Thank you to my author twin, Kate Bailey, for doing writing sprints with me and keeping me entertained during this process! I'm not sure I would've ever completed this book if it weren't for those many, many writing sprints.

To my launch team and my ARC readers, I appreciate you! Your support and encouragement keeps me going!

Also By

Under Kansas Skies series:
Running Mate, Madden and Odette's story.
House Mate, Drew and Sophie's story.
Check Mate, David and Isabella's story.
Cabin Mate, Brooks and Molly's story. (Available for preorder)!

About Author

Leah writes closed-door romance full of witty banter and lovable characters. She spends most of her time writing... and also petting her Maine Coon.

Although she's a Kansas girl at heart, Leah is a proud Air Force spouse and currently resides in Northern California with her husband and three children.

Her parents always told her she lived in her own little world and was oblivious to reality. The real world was simply too boring for Leah. Writing is how she enjoys sharing her little world with others.

www.ingramcontent.com/pod-product-compliance
Lightning Source LLC
Chambersburg PA
CBHW061609190726
48288CB00007B/2247

* 9 7 8 1 7 3 7 0 1 5 6 2 8 *